I0726955

Shenanigans
SERVING PARANORMALS
SINCE THE DARK AGES

SHIFTER
Shenanigans

SHIFTER SHENANIGANS

PEPPER MCGRAW

CONTENTS

PUBLISHING HISTORY
Shadows and Stars | Carter & Bradley Publishing | April 2018

Cover and inside images from Dreamtime:
Black Bear Illustration © Lkeskinen0
Cartoon girl © Subarashii21
Dragon Silhouette © Elena Kozyreva
Black Bear Walking © Sherry Piatti
A Glass of Beer © Leonora Adamchuk

ISBN 978-1-951247-20-1

Edited by J.L. Troughton
PMG Publishing

As PHOENIX SMITH hid behind Shenanigans' bar, the latest in her long string of waitress gigs, she remembered the claim she'd made to her new boss when he'd hired her two days before.

He'd warned her in his gravely voice that Shenanigans "doesn't have crowds like you're used to serving."

She'd assured him that she had plenty of experience working with the roughest of customers and that she could handle whatever his bar patrons threw at her.

Famous last words.

Phoenix peeked over the top of the bar and ducked back down, horrified. The brawl was still happening. Which wasn't a big deal. She'd been in barroom brawls before. Even knocked a few heads together herself when the occasion called for it.

The problem wasn't the fight.

It wasn't the beer bottles being thrown or the bodies flung through the air. It also wasn't the sounds of tables being destroyed or chairs knocked over.

The problem was that her boss, the unbelievably sexy bartender with the gravely voice, had lunged over the top of the bar and landed in a whole different body.

And then, in that *whole new body,* had let out a roar that shook the rafters and started tossing his customers everywhere.

And as for them.

Well, they were the problem too.

Snarling and growling, snapping at each other with viciously long fangs.

Fangs.

No, not like vampires.

More like werewolves. And werecougars. Which shouldn't even be a thing.

But since it was a thing, it also meant her boss was a werebear. Or wereblackbear.

This was crazy.

But now the location of this bar, which was right in the middle of the woods, with no roads leading up to it, made perfect sense to Phoenix.

At first, it had seemed crazy that people would hike to their neighborhood bar, but then the more she'd thought about it, the more she'd realized how ingenious it was. They'd never have to worry about drunk drivers because their customers could just walk their drunk asses home.

Only now she was realizing they'd probably be walking their drunk, *furry* asses home. Because who was more comfortable in the middle of the woods than a bunch of wolves and cougars?

Certainly not her. And now she was stuck here, with an unknown number of cougars and wolves between her and the door. Not to mention her boss, the scary-ass bear. What were the chances of her getting out of here without any of them noticing her?

Surely there was a back door. She couldn't believe she hadn't explored all the exits by now. She knew better than this.

"Shit, shit, shit. Phoenix, what are you going to do? Shit, this is madness!" She clutched her hair and dragged in a deep breath.

That's when she realized the sounds of fighting had stopped.

All the growls, snarls and roars had faded.

She'd never really understood how the hair on someone's neck could stand on end, but that's exactly what it did. Followed by a wave of ice-cold fear and a preternatural instinct that told her to run.

Only there was nowhere to go.

She'd trapped herself behind the bar.

"What's she doin' down there, Travis?" someone asked.

"Hell if I know."

Phoenix shivered at the sound of her boss's gravelly voice. If he was speaking, he had to be back in human form. Right?

She slowly raised her head and looked up.

The other two waitresses, along with the men and women they'd served that night, were all crowded around the bar, staring down at her.

While naked.

Okay, so she wasn't *positive* they were naked since the bar hid their lower halves, but everything up top was on display, so she had to assume…

"I thought you said you could handle this job," Travis growled at her as he shoved his way behind the bar. He faced her, hands on hips, a furious scowl on his face. "You told me you had experience with rough crowds. I knew I'd never heard of those bars before. They were all human bars, weren't they? You should have told me you'd never had any experience working at a shifter bar!"

Phoenix was speechless. It wasn't really what he was saying. Because she'd already pretty much processed that shifters were real and that this was a shifter bar. That had become shockingly clear when everyone in the bar went furry.

"Are you even listening to me?"

With great effort, Phoenix dragged her eyes away from the gorgeous cock bobbing in front of her and pushed to her feet. Swallowing, she looked her boss in the eye and said, "I'm sorry, what?"

"Why would you lie about your experiences? You could have been seriously hurt! At the very least, you should have shifted to give you a better chance in that brawl."

"Um, why exactly would I shift again?"

He stared at her, a perplexed look on his face, then glanced over at the customers, as if asking them for help.

"Well, usually, it's what shifters do, lass," one of the men offered.

She glanced at him. Then back at Travis.

She had no idea why they thought she was a shifter, but she wasn't about to admit the truth. They'd probably eat her or do something worse, like throw her in prison for the rest of her life, just to keep humans from discovering their secret.

"So why didn't you shift, honey?" Cassie, one of the other waitresses, asked.

"Yeah, why?"

Several voices chimed in, wondering what kind of shifter wouldn't even bother to shift for protection in the middle of a shifter brawl.

Phoenix didn't know what to say, so she just shrugged and refused to reply.

"What kind of shifter are you, anyway?"

"Karl!" Glory, another waitress, slapped him on the back of the head. "Never ask a woman about her animal!"

"Well, I never smelled her kind before."

"Me neither."

The murmurs of agreement spread.

Had they never been around humans before? Surely that wasn't possible.

"Doesn't matter," Glory insisted. "A woman's animal is very personal." She turned to Phoenix. "Don't worry about it, honey. You'll shift with us when you feel safe. Until then, you just keep your animal a well-guarded secret. No one will fault you for it." She glared around at the rest of the room. "Right?"

Travis rolled his eyes and crossed his arms, the movement causing his cock to bounce a little. "Look. You can't work in a shifter bar if you're not willing to shift. That's just the way it is."

"That's rather prejudicial," Phoenix said, glaring at him, trying desperately to ignore his bobbing cock. It couldn't be sanitary to have all that nakedness around – well, everything. And what was she saying? She should be taking this opportunity to quit, not arguing her right to stay.

"Oh, don't listen to him," Glory said. "I'm half-owner of this bar, Travis, and I say she stays."

This was news to Phoenix, who hadn't realized the waitress who'd been pitching in occasionally was one of the owners. She should have guessed when Travis introduced her as his sister though. It made sense that they would own the bar together.

"She did a magnificent job tonight," Glory continued. "And when the fight broke out, she quite sensibly retreated behind the bar, leaving you to knock sense into the lot of them."

"She's the best waitress we've had in a while, Travis," Cassie agreed. "We need her."

Travis groaned. "Whatever."

"You know, it'd be so much easier to take you seriously if your junk wasn't all out and proud right now." Phoenix waved a hand in the general vicinity of his cock. "Can you please put some clothes on? Or go to the other side of the bar? Or something? Nobody wants your pubes in their beer."

Groans and gagging sounds filled the air.

"Oh, my god, Travis, get away from there right now!" Glory exclaimed. "That is disgusting! I never even thought about that and now I'm going to have that vision in my head every damn time I order a beer from my own bar!"

Travis rolled his eyes. "It's not like I expected to explode out of my clothes tonight, Glory."

"Well, you should expect it," she said sharply. "It happens practically every weekend." She turned to face the customers still crowded around the bar. "All right. I think that's enough for one night. Clean up your areas, settle up your tabs and get out, the lot of you. And don't forget to tip your waitresses. *Generously*." She glared at them.

With shuffled feet and a number of muttered, "yes, ma'ams," the customers began to assist in the clean-up and one by one, wandered over to the bar to settle their tabs with Phoenix and Cassie.

An hour later, the doors were shut behind the final customer and thirty minutes after that, Phoenix was headed out the door, officially ending the weirdest shift she'd ever worked, and that was saying *a lot.*

2

As SOON AS the door closed behind Phoenix, Travis turned on his sister. "I can't believe you!"

Glory shrugged. "What?"

"A woman's animal is very personal." He mimicked her voice. "Since when?"

"Since you hired a waitress who freaked out when you shifted into a black bear."

"She's a shifter too!"

"Who still freaked out when you turned into a bear."

Travis groaned, remembering the sudden spike in Phoenix's scent. One minute, it had been a subtle blend of minty sweetness and the next it had become a wave of bitter fear. "I can't place her scent at all. It's driving my bear crazy."

"I know. She doesn't smell like prey though."

Travis wasn't exactly sure about that. She smelled unbelievably sweet to him. The scent had been driving him mad all night long. Every time she'd come up to the bar for a round of drinks, or even worse, had come *around* the bar to grab another bowl of peanuts, he'd had to restrain his bear, who'd desperately wanted to play with the pretty waitress.

When the bar fight had broken out, his bear had gone insane.

Phoenix had been standing at the bar when that damn cougar, Jerry, had transformed and lunged at one of the wolves. Phoenix hadn't even seemed to realize what was happening behind her, but Travis' bear had wasted no time in hurtling over the bar and getting between her and the insanity that ensued. Of course, that had been about the time when her scent had changed. Sometimes Travis hated being a bear, especially one living in the middle of wolf and cougar territories. The other shifters were always wary, as if they expected the bears to go on a rampage at any moment.

"I'm going for a run," Glory said, walking toward the door. "You coming?"

Travis shook his head. "Nah. I'm just gonna head on up."

"All right. See you tomorrow."

"See ya, sis."

Glory opened the door, then snapped, "What are you doing here?"

Travis tossed down the rag he'd been using to wipe down the bar and started to head around it when he heard Max's voice.

Rolling his eyes, he went back to what he'd been doing.

Max.

Beta for the local wolf pack.

Major pain in the ass.

And a constant source of amusement. His public pursuit of Glory provided endless entertainment for both the cougars and the wolves. Because Glory was having none of it.

"You figure out yet what animal your new waitress is hiding?"

Travis looked up, shocked to see that Glory was gone and Max was headed toward him. He couldn't believe she'd let that damn wolf inside! "We're closed," he growled.

"What about where she came from? And what pack, clan or den she belongs to?"

"She's not a wolf and that's all you need to know." Travis could feel his bear rising, unhappy with the questions being asked about his waitress. *Ours,* his bear rumbled.

"She chose not to shift in the middle of a shifter brawl. That tells me she's got something to hide, that she's running from something. Which means whatever she's running from might end up here one day. We need to know. If you don't want to ask her, that's fine. Between the cougars and my wolves, we'll figure it out."

A deep rumble poured from Travis' throat. "She's *my* waitress. I'll take responsibility for her. You wolves leave her alone."

Max raised an eyebrow. "You know none of the wolves *or* cougars are gonna let this go, right? It doesn't matter what either of us say, they're going to try to figure it out."

Travis groaned, his bear subsiding a little at that truth. There really was no getting around the rampant curiosity of shifters. And she'd smelled so intriguing, he really couldn't blame them for wondering. "As long as they treat her with respect, I'm good with them trying to figure it out."

Max grinned and rubbed his hands together. "This is gonna be fun."

Travis rolled his eyes. "Just remember. She's under my protection and if she gets hurt, my bear *will* destroy pretty much everything and everyone."

"Understood."

3

PHOENIX GOT BACK to the motel around two. Out of habit, she glanced at the clock and immediately calculated the nap she could take before having to get up for her shift at the diner, which began at six. Three glorious hours. She could sleep from now until five, at which point, she'd get up, take a shower, get ready and walk to work. Or she could sleep an extra thirty minutes and skip the shower.

Phoenix absolutely adored sleeping, especially when she could do it in small, *multiple* chunks of time. She loved sleeping so much that she arranged her life to accommodate her love of naps. An early morning shift at a restaurant, from six to eleven, and a night shift at a bar, from seven to one, were almost perfect hours, allowing her to sleep in two beautiful chunks of time between shifts.

Once though, she'd actually had *the* perfect schedule, where she'd had three short shifts at a diner and had managed to fit naps in between each shift. *Three naps a day!* It had been glorious. Sadly, she hadn't been able to replicate that schedule since.

Given how obsessed Phoenix was with her naps, she was rather shocked at how much she *wasn't* ready to lie down. She only had two hours and forty-five minutes left for napping, now that she'd wasted fifteen minutes staring into space. But even knowing that she was losing time in her dream space wasn't enough to make Phoenix turn out the lights.

Too much had happened this evening for her to just take a nap. She needed time to process.

Time to research shifters.

So, instead of taking a nap, Phoenix fired up her ancient laptop and began surfing the net.

An hour later, frustrated and annoyed, she gave up the task as impossible.

Romances – silly, funny, sexy, sometimes all three – and legends were all that she'd been able to find, which really shouldn't surprise her. After all, for most humans, shifters were just that – a legend.

Remembering how she had cowered behind the

bar and how furious Travis had been, she groaned and fell back onto the bed. She was going to have to grow a spine if she wanted to continue working at the bar.

Did she want to continue working there?

Shivering at the memory of Travis' voice, not to mention the glory that was the man naked – his chest alone about gave her palpitations and she'd seen a lot more than that – Phoenix knew she would not be abandoning the job at the bar. At least not yet.

This was the most interesting thing that had ever happened to her and she wasn't running away from it. Something inside her had come to life when she'd met Travis. It wasn't just his sexy looks, though his messy black hair and midnight eyes were quite captivating, not to mention his excessively gorgeous body. Still, it hadn't been his looks she'd noticed first. Instead it had been his scent. An amazing combination that reminded her both of the woods and of a crisp, winter night, she'd felt giddy after her first meeting with him. At first, the only thing that had kept her from pursuing that attraction was the fact that he was interviewing her for a job and then that he'd hired her, in effect becoming her boss. Now she had an even better reason – his scary-ass bear.

That feeling she'd had when she met him though – that clarity and awareness that brought everything into focus – wasn't something she'd ever experienced before. That it had happened again when everyone shifted at the bar was downright confusing. Maybe it was just the adrenaline that had caused her skin to tingle everywhere and all her senses to come on-line at once, but she figured anything that made her feel that alive had to be a good thing.

After years of feeling as if a shield of water stood between her and the world, somehow muting all her senses and leaving her sluggishly plodding forward, insulated from everything around her, this new sense of awareness was amazing. Even the panic she'd felt at the bar was better than the numbness she'd become accustomed to.

Glancing at the clock, Phoenix calculated that her two hours and forty-five minutes had now dwindled to ninety minutes. She'd wasted an hour and fifteen minutes reading legends and romance blurbs!

It was all that sexy bear's fault.

With a huff of exasperation, she set the alarm for five a.m., then hesitated and pushed it back to five-thirty. Forget the shower. Ninety minutes had just become two glorious hours.

She turned out the lights and almost instantly fell asleep, the vision of Travis lunging over the bar, his body transforming mid-flight from man to bear following her into her dreams.

The black bear spoke to her there, whispering secrets she couldn't quite hear, before eventually fading away. For a time, she simply drifted, but then eventually, like always, she slid into her dream space. It was dark, but cozy, and she was happy, curled in this place of warmth and safety. She could hear a soft and steady drum beating in the background and the world around her rocked gently to its beat.

Long, lazy moments later, the drumbeat strong and steady in her ears, she was curled high in a tree, reaching for something. Reaching…

Phoenix woke with a start.

That last part was new.

Not the tree.

She always ended her dream cradled in the branches of a tree.

The sense of longing though, of straining toward something, *that* was new.

What had she been reaching for?

Something wonderful.

Something that promised happiness.

Whatever it was though, it was gone, folded into the hazy memory of dreams.

~

Later that morning, as Phoenix bustled around the diner, working through the breakfast rush, waiting on the same customers she'd seen day in and day out since she'd begun working there the week before, she couldn't help but wonder how many of them were shifters.

If *all* of them were shifters.

"Order up," Jason called from the kitchen, breaking into her thoughts as she pondered whether the table of women by the door were shifters or plain ole humans like her.

About halfway through her shift, a group of men she recognized from Shenanigans the night before walked in and sat in her section, at the back of the diner.

She wasn't sure if they were wolves or cougars or a mix, but she remembered settling their tab at the very end of the night, so they'd definitely been there when the fight broke out.

"Hey, there," one of them greeted her with a huge grin. "You work here too, eh?"

"Sure do. What can I get you guys?"

"Phoenix, right?" one of the other men asked.

"That's right."

"I'm Max," he said. "This is our alpha, Adam." He gestured to the man across from him. "And Pete, Sam and Karl." He pointed to each of the guys as he said their names.

Phoenix could feel her eyes widening. She couldn't believe they actually had an alpha, like real wolves did. Or maybe they were cougars. Did cougars have alphas? Her breath hitched and she carefully let it out before speaking. "It's nice to meet all of you. Do you know what you want or do you need a minute?"

After taking their orders, Phoenix made a circuit of her tables on the way back to the front, where she handed her orders into the kitchen and worked on grabbing drinks and refills. She then worked her way back in reverse, ending at their table again.

"So, Phoenix," Max said as she began passing out drinks, "you part of their pack?"

Only years of experience working in bars and diners kept Phoenix from fumbling the drinks at his question. "Um. What? Whose pack?" She glanced around quickly, shocked they were even discussing this at the diner. Were they all shifters here too?

"Ah, don't worry about the humans," Pete said.

"Yeah, they're too far away to hear us," Sam said.

Phoenix glanced around again, noting the people at the tables closest to theirs and wondering if the women by the door were humans after all, since they were the farthest away.

"So are you part of the Phoenix pack?" Max asked again. "You know, since you carry their name and all."

Phoenix just stared at him for a minute, then said quietly, "Phoenix is the name of at least 15 different places worldwide, not to mention it's a mythical bird that rises from the ashes. Why would you assume my name comes from a pack?" Without waiting for an answer, she walked away.

"Tricky," she heard one of the men mutter.

"Do you think she might actually *be* a phoenix?" another one whispered.

Thank goodness she was walking away because Phoenix knew the shock she felt was written all over her face. She wanted to go back and ask if there really were phoenix shifters, but she couldn't afford to draw attention to her own ignorance. Surely, if she were a shifter, she'd know that already. This was like being tortured! She had so many questions and no way to get them answered.

When the men had finished eating and she brought them their check, Adam spoke for the first time. "You have an alpha that's going to be looking for you?"

Phoenix looked him in the eye and told him the truth, "No, sir. No one's looking for me at all." She had no idea why she'd admitted that and was honestly horrified that she'd just told a group of shifters that she could disappear without a trace and no one would even notice.

Adam just nodded. "It's not a deal-killer, but things do get a bit complicated when you get too many alphas in one territory. And we always like some advance warning." He stared at her. "If that changes, I expect you to let us know."

Phoenix nodded. "It won't." How could it when she wasn't a shifter? When she had no family, let alone a pack like they did?

"All right then. Welcome to Jamesville, Phoenix. We're always happy to have new shifter residents." He stood, dropped a wad of cash on the table, patted her on the shoulder and headed for the front door. The rest of the men stood and murmured their own welcome messages to her as they trooped past.

Dragging in a breath, Phoenix began to clear the table. She didn't understand why they were so convinced that she was a shifter. It seemed unlikely at best. Wouldn't she know by now? Wouldn't she have shifted at least once in her life if she was capable of such a thing?

She wished she knew more about shifters.

She wished she knew more about her birth family.

As she worked the last hour of her shift, Phoenix tried not to think about the possibility of being a shifter. It just wasn't possible.

She could never be that lucky.

4

WHEN PHOENIX WALKED out of the diner around eleven that morning, she found Travis waiting for her. He was leaning against a black pickup and her heart gave a thud when she saw him.

He pushed away from the truck and walked toward where she stood, frozen on the sidewalk.

"What are you doing here?"

"One of the wolves called me. Told me you were working here too. You must be exhausted."

She shrugged. "It's a short shift."

"Do you have to come back later?"

"No. They have others for the lunch and dinner shifts."

He nodded. "How many days are you working here?"

"Six. It's not so bad. I have Sundays off."

"Yeah, but you're working at the bar four nights a week."

"I know."

"Darlin', there's no way you can keep that kind of schedule going long-term."

She shrugged. "I do it all the time. I'll be fine. They're both short shifts. I get off here at eleven and I don't have to be at the bar until seven tonight."

He sighed. "All right. Well, at least let me give you a ride home."

"I have a car, you know."

"Is it here?"

She stared at him. It wasn't. She didn't usually bother with the car when the weather was nice, but how did he know that?

"Well?"

She sighed. "No, but–"

"Do you really prefer to walk right now?"

Honestly, she didn't. "Fine. Let's just go. I'm ready for a nap." Which was the only reason she agreed. Getting back sooner meant she could take a longer nap.

He barked out a laugh. "I bet. All right. Come on."

When they arrived at the hotel, though, she regretted agreeing to the ride.

"This place is a dump, darlin'." Travis glared at the front sign that had probably at one time said HOTEL, but that now just said H___EL.

Phoenix actually really liked that sign, as she felt it was a fairly accurate description of what one could expect on the inside. She wasn't going to mention that to Travis though.

"It's not that bad," Phoenix said. "On the plus side, it's really cheap. And I don't have to sign a lease." This last point was the real reason Phoenix had chosen the hotel. She preferred not to commit to a specific amount of time in any one place and now that she knew this town was full of shifters, that seemed more important than ever. The importance of being able to leave at a moment's notice couldn't be overstated.

"You should move in with us."

"What?"

"There are three apartments above the bar. Glory has one and I have the other. The third one's pretty small, but compared to where you're staying, it'll probably feel like the Ritz."

"No, no, no, no, no." Phoenix shook her head.

"Let's get your stuff." He strode toward the front door of the building.

Phoenix raced after him. "No, Travis. You don't have to do this."

He ignored her as he crossed the lobby and came to a stop in front of the elevator. He glared at the out of order sign, then turned and demanded, "What floor?"

"Four," Phoenix squeaked out, horrified that once again, she was sharing info she really shouldn't with a complete stranger. What was it about these men and about Travis in particular? It seemed all he had to do was look at her and all her brain cells died!

"Let's go." He led the way up the stairs, ranting all the while. "I'd be surprised if there were two residents in this entire place and you're up on the fourth floor? Forcing you to walk up all these stairs at two o'clock in the morning after a long night at the bar. I don't think so." On and on he went, ranting about the state of the lighting, the sagging stairs, the crumbling railing, the peeling wallpaper, the water spots on the ceiling.

"I had no idea you were such a prima donna, Travis," Phoenix teased when they finally reached her door.

He growled in response.

Which if Phoenix was being honest, she found unbelievably sexy. That he could growl. Like his bear. In human form. She wanted to ask him to do it again, but he looked so pissed she decided maybe she should wait on that.

It didn't take her long to pack her stuff. She didn't have much. A backpack and a suitcase and she was done.

"That's it?"

"I have a few things in my car, but yeah, mostly this is it."

"Let's go."

"I have to check out."

"Oh, we'll get you checked out." He led the way back downstairs, ranting all the while, "You should never have been checked into this place to begin with. It should have been shut down years ago." He stopped at the second floor landing to glare over his shoulder at her. "How much are you paying for this dump anyway?"

"Eighty bucks a week." Harry'd wanted almost double that, but Phoenix didn't think Travis needed to know that.

Travis grunted. "You all paid up?"

"I'm supposed to pay rent for the week on Saturdays, so I owe him for today."

Travis just shook his head and stomped down the last flight of stairs.

When they got to the lobby, he informed Harry that Phoenix was moving out and she handed over her room key.

"This morning was on the house," Travis said. "Consider it payment for her having to walk four flights of stairs instead of using the elevator all week."

Harry looked like he wanted to protest, but one look from Travis and he subsided. "That's fine. Take care, Phoenix."

"You too, Harry."

Phoenix followed Travis out to the parking lot, where he stored her suitcase in the bed of his truck.

"That your car?" He nodded toward her blue Honda Civic.

"Yeah, that's mine."

"All right. Just follow me."

"Wait. Where are we going?"

"Back to the bar to get you moved into the apartment."

"But how? There aren't any roads up there."

Travis just stared at her. "Did you *walk* to the bar last night?"

"Well, yeah."

"So when you left the bar this morning…"

"I walked back here, yeah." She hadn't exactly enjoyed the walk. Even with her flashlight, and the bright light of the moon, the woods were pretty creepy at night.

"Did any of the guys see you shift?"

She just stared at him.

"Yeah. I guess they were probably all gone by the time you left. Too bad. I have a feeling they're going to be hounding you to find out what your animal is."

Phoenix just rolled her eyes.

"Anyway, that's a pretty long walk, even in animal form with night vision. You should have asked one of us for a ride."

Phoenix shook her head. "What do you mean a ride? There's no parking lot, no roads."

Travis laughed. "Actually, there *is* a road *and* a small parking lot at the back of the bar. Come on. Follow me and I'll show you."

Phoenix huffed. "Do you mean to tell me that when I walked to and from the bar last night, it wasn't necessary?"

"Guess so, yeah."

"Why didn't you tell me there was a parking lot?"

"Darlin', I assumed you knew. In fact, I assumed

you drove to the interview. It just didn't even occur to me."

She sighed. "Whatever. Let's go." She stomped over to her car and climbed in. She couldn't believe no one had even mentioned the parking lot! She'd put the address into her phone and the phone had actually said, "There are no roads leading to this destination." Then it had given her walking directions. Which now that she thought about it made no sense. If the bar had an address, that meant there had to be a road. Right?

She followed Travis out of the motel parking lot and down the outer road that ran along the outskirts of town. About five minutes into the drive, he slowed and turned left directly into the woods. She followed him onto a narrow passage that wasn't so much a road as it was a gravel path. They stayed on that road for about five minutes, then turned onto another one that quickly opened up into a small parking lot.

"Unbelievable."

She pulled in and parked next to his truck and stared. If the bar was nearby, she couldn't tell. The parking lot was completely surrounded by woods.

If she was about to get eaten, she probably deserved it. This was about the stupidest thing she'd ever done, following a virtual stranger deep into the woods. This was how horror movies began!

A knock on the window made her jump, then giggle. She turned off the car and opened the door. If he was going to kill her, at least she'd have the comfort of knowing that her killer was sexy as hell.

She climbed out.

"You okay?"

"Yeah." She nodded. "Where's the bar?"

"Right through there." He pointed to the woods in front of them, but if there was a path, she couldn't see it. "You have everything you need?"

"Oh, um, just a minute." She grabbed her backpack and purse form the backseat, locked the car and turned to him. He already had her suitcase, so they were ready. "Lead the way."

There really was a path! It was even paved. You had to be straight on to see it since the trees and bushes blocked its view from the sides, but it was there.

It was about a three minute walk through the woods to reach the back of the bar, but that was so much better than the thirty minute walk she'd taken through the woods to get to the motel.

Unbelievable.

The apartment Travis showed her was actually

quite cute. It was just one big room with a small galley kitchen and a bathroom, but it was perfect. It was already furnished with a king-sized bed, a dresser, a small sitting area and a flat screen TV. "Wow. This really is the Ritz compared to where I was."

"Good. I'm glad you like it. I'll leave you to get unpacked, but before I go, we should talk."

"What? Oh. Of course. We didn't discuss rent."

Travis made an exasperated sound. "Not what we need to talk about. The apartment was empty anyway. Consider it a perk of the job."

"No, no, no." Phoenix shook her head. "Absolutely not."

He groaned. "Fine. How about you help me Tuesday afternoons in exchange for rent? That's when my stock gets delivered and I have to do inventory. It's a terrible job and Glory refuses to help."

"Okay, sure. I work at the diner until 11, but I should be able to help after that."

"Perfect."

"So what did you want to talk about then?"

"Your animal. What kind is it?"

PHOENIX APPEARED STUNNED at his question. "Why should I tell you?"

"Sweetheart, in case you didn't notice, this is shifter territory. Yeah, there are a few humans around, but mostly on the whole, this mountain's ours. And you don't just waltz into shifter territory without announcing yourself."

Phoenix raised an eyebrow. "I rather thought applying for jobs in the community was a pretty good way of announcing myself."

"Maybe. If your animal weren't so elusive. And if we knew where you'd come from."

"You have my application. You know exactly where I've worked for the last ten years."

"True. I also know that you've bounced from territory to territory that entire time. So from that, do I assume you're a loner with no clan, no pack, no den at your back?"

Phoenix looked defensive. "How'd you know I was a shifter anyway?"

What the hell kind of question was that? He stared at her, stunned. If he couldn't smell her animal right then, he'd think she was human. "What do you mean how'd I know? How did you know you were working at a shifter bar? How'd you know I was a black bear?"

She just stared at him.

He was getting a really weird feeling about this. "Shit. You did know that you'd applied to a shifter bar, right?"

Phoenix didn't answer.

Fuck. Travis dragged a hand through his hair and groaned. No wonder she'd freaked out in the bar. "So I'm guessing your animal doesn't have a finely developed sense of smell." Which was totally weird. "I don't even know what animal that would be." He raised an eyebrow. "Care to enlighten me?"

When Phoenix didn't answer, he huffed in exasperation. "So I'm guessing you wouldn't have applied if you'd known we were shifters, which tells me what? Are you on the run? Can we expect enforcers to show up in a couple days, trying to track your ass down?"

Phoenix rolled her eyes. "I already told Adam that no one is looking for me."

Adam. When had she met that fucker? "How the hell did you meet him?"

"He came into the diner for breakfast this morning."

And of course he'd interrogated her right away. Fuckin' alphas.

"So you can smell my animal?"

"What?"

"My animal. You can smell it?"

Travis stared at her, a little disoriented at the way she'd called her animal "it". "Yeah, I can smell her. She's subtle, sometimes even barely there. She's really good at hiding herself." A thought suddenly struck him. "Maybe even of disguising herself?"

Phoenix looked surprised, so maybe not. Her animal must just be a type they'd never encountered before.

Travis sighed. "Are you ever going to share your animal with us?"

She shrugged.

He winced. If she came to the bar with that attitude, it would be like waving a red flag in front of a whole herd of bulls. "Just don't be surprised if the entire bar gets involved in trying to identify your animal. Like all shifters, they're a curious bunch. Even worse though, they're highly competitive. The wolves will want to figure it out first and the cougars will want the same."

"I'm not worried about it."

Her scent said exactly the opposite though. It had slowly strengthened during their conversation and was now a mix of worry, anxiety and fear. He couldn't figure out why it mattered though. If she wasn't on the run, if no one was after her, why did she care if a bunch of shifters knew her animal side? He didn't want her bolting though so he tried to reassure her.

He stepped into her space, slid one hand around the back of her neck and settled the other on her shoulder, then leaned his forehead into hers. "They know you're under my protection, Phoenix, so you really don't have to worry. You'll be safe here."

The scent of her anxiety fled on a wave of arousal and his bear lunged forward, licking at the air like he could taste her honey. Christ.

He started to pull away, but she reached up and

caught his wrists in her hands and stared into his eyes.

"God, you're so beautiful," he muttered and then he did what he'd been imagining ever since she walked into his bar earlier that week and applied for the open waitress position. He kissed her.

6

ONE MINUTE PHOENIX was worrying about what would happen if – *when* – the shifters discovered she had no animal, the next she was drowning in waves of heat.

She gasped as Travis claimed her mouth, sweeping inside and capturing her tongue with his. All thoughts evaporated as she clutched his shoulders and lost herself in his kiss.

Long, drugging minutes later, he released her lips to trail kisses along her jaw to her neck, at which point his arms closed around her convulsively and he pulled her tight to his body, burying his face in her neck and inhaling deeply.

She wondered if she smelled as amazing to him as he did to her. His woodsy scent had intensified with every kiss until her head swam with the headiness of it.

"I wonder if your animal's napping?" he asked.

"What?" She pulled away to stare at him.

"She's really subtle, barely there at all. I wondered if she's curled up, taking a nap."

Just those words made Phoenix shiver with desire. She could almost imagine how wonderful it would be. Curled up, napping in her dream space, Travis curled around her, holding her safe.

"Ah," Travis said, a satisfied rumble in his voice. "There she is."

"What?"

"Your animal's peeking at me from your eyes." He cupped her cheeks and stared deeply. "There you are, sweet love. Don't be shy."

A little freaked out, Phoenix blinked a couple times.

Travis sighed. "Ah, well. Maybe next time." He kissed her gently. "No worries, darlin'. I've got tons of patience. I'll coax her out." He spoke without lifting his lips from hers, punctuating the end of each sentence with a firm kiss.

After one last, heat-filled kiss that swamped all her senses, Travis finally pulled away. "I know you must be exhausted, so I'll leave you to your nap." He walked to the door. "If you need anything, my apartment's across the way and Glory's is at the end of the hall. It's Glory's night to cook if you want to join us. We'll eat at her place at four." And with that, he was gone.

After that, it took a while for Phoenix to settle enough to actually enjoy her nap. This had never happened before. In the past, her dream state was only ever seconds away. She'd curl up or lie down and in seconds would be happy and warm.

But today, every time she was about to find that place, the memory of Travis' kisses would ignite a flash of heat and her dream state would slip away as desire engulfed her. She had to call upon the meditation techniques she'd developed while living in foster homes growing up, techniques that had kept her sane while living in impossible situations, surrounded by people she didn't trust.

It had been a long time since she'd needed to meditate before napping. The moment she'd been free of the state's care, she'd begun a slow but steady progression upward until one day she'd slid into her dream state the moment her head hit the pillow and she'd not needed to meditate since.

Today though. Today that sexy bartender had

completely eradicated years of work and her dream state had never seemed so far away.

After long minutes of deep breathing and other exercises to blank her mind, Phoenix finally managed to relax enough that she was able to spend ninety-five glorious minutes napping before her alarm cut through the soft beat of the drum and woke her.

As she got ready for the evening and her bar shift, Phoenix pondered her dream. There had been no reaching this time. Just the same dream as always, the same sensation of sleeping curled somewhere safe and warm, listening to the soft beat of drums. And she wondered as she always did, where this place was that she dreamed of and who played the drums she heard there. Knowing there were no answers to these questions, for she'd had them as long as she could remember, Phoenix relegated them to the back of her mind and left her apartment.

A few seconds later, she stood outside the door to Glory's apartment and tried to convince herself to knock. She wasn't sure what she was doing there. Sure, Travis had invited her, but she wasn't sure she really wanted to continue building connections with him or his sister. They believed she was a shifter too and she just didn't know how she felt about that. She was afraid to hope and she was worried about their reaction if they were wrong. Would they hate her if she was only human?

At that moment, the door swung open and Travis grinned at her. "You ever going to knock?"

Phoenix shrugged. "How'd you know I was here?"

"I keep forgetting your animal doesn't have the same sense of smell most shifters do. Which is really kind of weird when you think about it."

"Oh, don't listen to him." Glory shoved her brother aside and grabbed Phoenix's arm. "Come on in, Phoenix. I'm so happy you decided to join us and I'm especially glad you agreed to move into the empty apartment." She led Phoenix through a spacious living space into an even larger kitchen that smelled amazing. "Have a seat." She waved a hand at a bar stool that stood on one side of a huge kitchen island. "We've talked about renting out the apartment before, but it's so small, we weren't sure any shifter would ever want to live there. And of course, we'd never offer it to a human."

Phoenix winced and was glad Glory wasn't looking at her, but instead was bustling around the kitchen, grabbing bowls and filling them with the delicious smelling meal she'd been preparing.

Though it wasn't a great beginning, the rest of the afternoon was lovely. Glory had a fabulous sense of humor and Travis was super attentive, asking lots of questions that of course, Phoenix did her best to deflect. He asked about where she'd lived and she entertained them with stories of the different bars she'd worked in all over the country.

When he asked why she chose to work with full humans, she just shrugged and said, "It was less complicated that way." She didn't even know why it would be less complicated to work in a human bar, but it seemed the sort of thing that might be true.

Travis nodded. "I'm sure it's easier to handle brawling humans than shifters. And even though you didn't know you were applying to a shifter bar, I'm glad you did. You could have gone to the full human bar the next town over."

And she probably would have had she only known. "Yeah, but this was closer."

She was trying hard not to actually lie to Glory and Travis. After all, they were super nice and had taken a chance, both in giving her a job and in letting her stay in the apartment. At the same time, she wasn't sure it was the best idea she'd ever had, taking them up on either offer.

And how could she possibly pursue whatever was

happening between her and Travis when he didn't even really know her?

Thankfully she didn't have much time to worry about it because six o'clock came quickly and before she knew it, they had to be downstairs prepping the bar to open.

As the night wore on, the bar became more and more crowded and it wasn't long before Phoenix realized Travis was right. The wolves and cougars were going to do their best to figure out her beast. That was okay though because she figured as long as they were trying to guess it, there was no chance of them realizing she didn't have one.

Every time she took an order or brought drinks to a table, some wolf or cougar would try to guess her animal. Every animal you could think of. Phoenix just kept shaking her head because of course, no matter what they guessed, they were always wrong. No matter what Travis thought he'd seen in her eyes.

If she was a shifter, she'd know it.

Maybe she was being a little stubborn. After all, she'd grown up in foster care without any knowl-edge of her real family, but still. From what she'd seen of these shifters, stress, anger, frustration and even laughter could make them experience an unplanned shift or partial shift. One of the cougars got to laughing uncontrollably and a bunch of whiskers popped out of his cheeks, which just caused more laughter and more whiskers to appear.

Not to mention that when the cougars drank too much, they had a tendency to go full-on cat and take naps under the tables (something Phoenix completely related to, even though alcohol was never a requirement in her case). And when the wolves got drunk, they tended to howl. A lot.

The more Phoenix learned about these shifters and the more she got to know them, the more she wished it wasn't true. That she wasn't human. That they were right and she did have an animal hiding somewhere deep inside. Unfortunately, she was pretty sure she would have shifted at least once as a child and especially as a teenager, living in the stressful environments she had. Which meant she was human. Depressingly, boringly human.

"Unicorn," one of the cougars guessed as she set down his beer.

"Seriously, Cole?" Another cougar rolled his eyes. "I'm pretty sure we'd have heard about unicorn shifters."

"You never know!" Cole exclaimed. "I mean, there aren't that many animals whose scent I wouldn't recognize. I bet it's the same for you, Dan. I think unicorn makes perfect sense."

Phoenix just shook her head and headed to the next table where a bunch of wolves were hanging out.

"I was right, wasn't I?" Pete, one of the wolves from the diner earlier that day, asked.

"Right about what?"

"You're named for your animal, aren't you? The cat actually makes sense. Of course, we wouldn't recognize the scent of a mythical creature. But it's not a unicorn. It's a phoenix, right?"

"I was named for the city I was found in, not for the animal I can shift into." Phoenix handed him his whisky and walked away.

"Wait, what does that mean? Found in?"

Shit. Phoenix ignored his question and hurried back to the bar to get another round of drinks.

She couldn't believe she'd revealed something so personal. All the questions were starting to get to her though. Everyone had agreed that she wasn't a bear, a cat or a wolf, simply because they were all certain they'd recognize that scent. This seemed to be the only thing they agreed on though. They pretty much argued about everything else, insisting that she could be almost any other animal (though no one suggested human).

And so the guesses kept coming, making her sadder as the night wore on, because she was pretty sure she wasn't a buffalo, moose, elk, deer, fox, raccoon, squirrel, opossum or any of the other animals they'd suggested.

"You okay?" Travis asked as she set her empty tray on top of the bar.

She nodded.

"Don't worry. They'll give up after a while."

She forced a smile. "It's fine. They're just having some fun."

He studied her for a minute, then shook his head. "They don't get to make you sad though." He started to untie his bar apron. "I'll make them stop."

"No, it's fine." If he made them stop, they might wonder why.

"Are you sure?"

"Yeah. It's fine."

He leaned over the bar, caught the back of her neck, pulled her close and kissed her.

Heat swamped Phoenix as she clutched his shoulders and kissed him back.

The whistles and howls of cougars and wolves eventually broke them apart.

"What was that for?" Phoenix breathed softly, inhaling his incredible scent and savoring his taste on her lips and tongue.

He grinned. "Just letting them know you're mine. In every way."

That statement should have annoyed Phoenix. She belonged to no one but herself. Instead, it made her feel warm and safe. Protected in a way she'd never really felt before. Smiling, she turned and walked back to her tables, handing out beers and drinks and taking new orders as she went, the pestering and questions about her animal no longer penetrating the fog of comfort that surrounded her.

Later that night, Travis left Phoenix at her door after a long round of kisses and caresses and extreme petting that left her gasping for breath and horny as hell. She came so close to inviting him in. The only thing that held her back was how different they were and her fear that he'd be disappointed if he knew she was only human.

7

TRAVIS WASN'T SURE why he hadn't pushed for more with Phoenix.

He was pretty certain a little more coaxing would have gotten him into her apartment and then he'd finally be able to taste her sweet honey, something his bear demanded pretty much every time they were in her presence.

But he knew she wasn't ready. Her animal was still hiding from him and until she revealed herself, he couldn't be certain what their true path was. Until then, he'd be patient. Even if it killed him.

Phoenix wasn't scheduled to work at the bar again until Wednesday, which gave him a full three days to court her animal in privacy without those interfering cougars and wolves around. Surely he could coax her out by then.

Famous last words.

Three days later, he still had no idea what Phoenix's animal was and even more frustrating, she was hiding from him again. He hadn't caught a glimpse of her in the three days they'd spent together, not even on Sunday, when the bar was closed and they'd had the entire day to spend together.

Travis had taken her on a hike in the woods to one of his favorite spots and she'd practically melted when she'd seen the waterfall. They'd kissed and made out and played in the water in human form and she'd been completely relaxed with him and so happy. He'd been sure she'd share her animal then, but nothing. What kind of animal was faced with the beauty of that waterfall and didn't want to shift to play in it? He'd think she was a cat, but the cougars swore she had no feline in her.

The next two days she'd worked at the diner and he'd worked at the bar, so their time together had been significantly shortened. Still they'd had fun, cooking dinner together one night and completing inventory together the next afternoon. Then, later that same night, she'd actually hung out in the bar for a while, just keeping him company. Of course, the damn cougars and wolves had started their guessing games again, but this time she hadn't seemed as bothered by it. She'd just laughed and let them guess and never answered one way or the other.

It was driving him and his bear crazy. Why was it such a big secret?

The guesses grew wilder as the night wore on because after all, the fact that it was a secret made everyone think it had to be something no one had ever seen before.

"T-Rex?" Karl guessed.

"Don't you think she'd be a little bigger if she was a T-Rex?" Pete scoffed.

"You never know."

Phoenix just rolled her eyes and ignored them all.

At the end of the night, they had their usual incredibly sexy make-out session in the entryway of her apartment.

Travis backed her into the wall, hitched her legs around his waist and devoured her mouth. She tasted so unbelievably sweet and spicy all at the same time. He ground himself against her, rubbing her in just the right spot, fingers of his right hand rolling and pinching a nipple while his other hand cupped and squeezed her bottom, holding her tight against him.

When he finally pulled away, he was rewarded by the sight of her animal peeking at him from her gorgeous brown eyes. Her pupils had elongated, forming vertical slits with a tiny ring of gold surrounding them, and her eye color had darkened to a deep and unrelenting black.

"Ah, my love, there you are," he whispered, leaning his forehead against hers and staring into her eyes. "Come out and play with me, yeah?"

Of course, right then, Travis' bear stretched and peeked out through his own eyes and just like that, she was gone.

He huffed in exasperation. Stupid bear. Always so impatient.

"Um, Travis, I don't think–" Phoenix sighed, a look of unhappiness on her face.

Travis kissed her and said, "Don't worry so much, my sweet. Your animal will come out when she feels safe and that's just fine."

"Yeah, but…" Phoenix hesitated, then blurted out, "what if she never comes out?"

Travis pulled back. "Of course, she'll come out, sweetheart. We just have to be patient."

Phoenix looked away, making him reconsider his words.

"What makes you think she won't?"

Phoenix shrugged, but Travis was beginning to realize that her shrugs had a wealth of meaning to them.

"She *has* come out for you before, right?"

Phoenix didn't answer.

Shit. Was she latent?

Travis carried her further into the apartment and settled into an armchair with her facing him, legs straddling his. "Come on, sweetheart. I won't judge you." He smoothed her hair away from her face and stared into her eyes. "Have you ever shifted into your animal?"

Phoenix's eyes slid away from his.

"No, sweetheart, stay looking at me."

Her eyes slid back.

"Please tell me the truth. Have you ever shifted?"

8

———

THE MOMENT HAD come and Phoenix wasn't ready.

Travis deserved to know the truth though.

She shook her head.

"You've never shifted."

"No."

"Are you latent then?"

"What's latent?"

"It's shifters who have an animal inside, but for whatever reason, the animal can't get out."

Phoenix sighed. She really didn't want have to tell him this. "I'm not latent, Travis."

He looked confused.

"I'm human."

Travis laughed. "No, you're not."

"Yes, I am. Look. I know it's hard to accept, but I'm not a shifter. I've never had an animal, I'm just me."

"That's not possible. I can smell your animal, Phoenix. What makes you think you're not a shifter? What happened to your pack or clan or whatever?"

"I don't have one. I grew up in foster care."

"Hold up. Do you mean *human* foster care?"

Phoenix nodded.

"How the hell'd that happen?"

"I was found at the scene of a car accident in Phoenix – the city, not the pack – when I was a toddler. That's where my name came from. My parents were killed in the accident and they couldn't find any relatives. So I went into the system."

"Which meant what exactly?"

Phoenix shrugged. "I was moved around a lot, from one foster family to the next. They were all given money to take care of me and when they didn't want me anymore, they'd send me back."

"Back where?"

"To the state. And then I'd get sent to the next family."

"So you were raised by humans."

"Exactly."

"I don't understand how this happened," he

growled. "Where was your clan, your pack? How could they just abandon you?"

"Travis." Though he was starting to understand, he still refused to see. "I don't have one. I'm *human*."

"Okay. I understand why you think that, Phoenix, and now I understand why your animal's been hiding. She's never been around shifters before, not for any length of time anyway. If she had, she probably would have shifted by now."

"Travis–"

"I know you don't believe me, Phoenix, but I promise you." He cupped her face in his hands and leaned his forehead against hers. "You *are* a shifter."

"But what if I'm not?" The look on his face made her add hastily, "Or what if I'm latent? What if I never shift, Travis?"

"Then you never shift." He sounded matter-of-fact, but she could tell the thought of it worried him. "It doesn't change how I feel about you."

She relaxed a little, sensing his sincerity. Yes, he was worried, but if it truly wouldn't change his feelings for her, then she wasn't going to worry about it.

"Wait a minute." He jerked upright, a stunned look on his face. "Does this mean when everyone shifted in the bar…" his voice trailed away.

She smiled at him and waited.

"Was that the first time you ever saw anyone shift?"

"Yep. It was also when I found out that shifters exist."

"You didn't even know—of course, you didn't. You thought you were just human, right? All this time. You never even knew you had an animal inside."

"I'm still not convinced."

"I know, sweetheart. Don't worry though. I promise we'll figure this out. Besides, once the cougars and wolves hear about this—"

"Wait. You're going to tell them?"

"Of course. They might be able to help."

Phoenix was horrified. This was exactly what she'd been trying to avoid. "They don't like humans!"

"What makes you say that?"

"Glory said you wouldn't rent the apartment to a human and the—"

"Because a human would discover we exist, not because we hate them."

"But what if I'm right and I am human? What will they do to me?"

"Nothing, sweetheart. It's rare, but we have had the occasional human-shifter mating and there are a few trustworthy humans who know the truth about us. I promise, Phoenix, even if you were human, *which you're not,* I would protect you, and so would they."

She sighed. He looked so sincere. "Fine," she muttered, not at all convinced, but willing to trust him for now.

"Besides, the wolves and cougars might be able to help us coax out your animal."

Phoenix couldn't imagine anything would make that happen, but she didn't have the heart to burst Travis' bubble.

9

"SO YOU MEAN to tell me you really *could* be a phoenix?" Pete demanded.

Max huffed in amusement. When Travis had called the pack earlier that day to share that Phoenix had no idea what her animal was, Pete had immediately started in on his absurd theory again. He'd been impatiently waiting all day, just so he could have this chance to ask that question.

"What? No." Phoenix rolled her eyes.

"How do you know? I mean, you said you don't know what your animal is, so maybe you are. Maybe *that's* why you're named Phoenix."

"I highly doubt the humans gave me the name of a mythical bird because they thought I was one too,

Pete. It's just like I said. I was named Phoenix because that's where I was found."

Pete sighed. "Well, that's not as interesting, now is it?"

"No, but she could still be a unicorn," Cole called from the next table over.

Phoenix just shook her head and walked away.

The minute she was gone, Glory appeared at Max's side. "We need a plan, boys." She grabbed a chair and shoved her way in between him and Karl.

Since she never willingly spent time with Max, he could only stare in amazement.

"What?" she demanded.

He shook his head. "Nothing, nothing."

"What do you mean we need a plan? For what?" Pete asked.

"Yeah, for what?" the others chimed in.

"My brother's seriously into Phoenix and you know how bears are."

"He's already attached," Max guessed. Bears. They were stupid stubborn.

"And he's not going to let her go, even if her animal never comes out."

Pete shrugged. "So? They're a cute couple. What do you care?"

Cole reached across the aisle and slapped Pete's head.

"Hey!" Pete whirled on Cole with a growl. "Knock it off, cat!"

"Well, don't be stupid," Cole said. "You know how bears are about their mates."

"Yeah, so they're attached. I don't see the big deal."

Glory sighed. "If she never shifts, he'll never know for certain. His *bear* will never know for certain."

"Seriously?" Pete asked. "I knew the second I met Jenny that she was mine. Didn't matter what her wolf or mine said. Luckily they both agreed, but still."

"Bears are different," Glory said.

"She's right," Cole said as he swung his chair around and shoved his way into their space. "If she never shifts, his bear won't ever be truly happy because it won't feel like a true mating to him."

"That sucks." Dan stood up from his table and wandered over to join them.

"Seriously?" Max demanded. "Where are all these cougars coming from?"

"Even if it's a true mating?" Dan ignored Max to ask Glory.

"Even if," Glory said. "A part of his bear will always be holding back and she'll know it. Even if she never shifts, her animal will sense that his animal has rejected her and they'll both be miserable."

"So what are we going to do?" Karl asked.

"We need a plan," Glory repeated. "A plan to get Phoenix to shift."

Max winced. He figured there was zero chance this wouldn't get out of hand fast.

10

TRAVIS DIDN'T LIKE the way Glory joined the wolves and he especially didn't like it when one by one, the cougars wandered over as well. They were up to something. Especially based on the speculative looks they kept giving Phoenix.

Of course, he knew his sister would never hurt Phoenix, but he also knew Glory was worried. Worried that Phoenix might never shift. Worried that her brother's bear might never have the true mating it deserved.

Under those circumstances, she might be willing to do anything.

He was relieved when the night was finally over

and he was able to usher everyone out and turn his full attention to Phoenix.

Cassie had cashed out thirty minutes before last call, and Glory, to his shock, left with the wolves, leaving him and Phoenix to close the bar on their own. Which wasn't a big deal. He enjoyed stealing kisses from her as they worked side-by-side wiping everything down, loading the dishwasher and sweeping the floor.

As they worked, Travis contemplated his next steps. Now that he knew Phoenix's animal wasn't necessarily hiding from him *or* his bear, he was rethinking his whole strategy. If as he suspected, Phoenix's animal had never appeared because it had no shifter connections, holding back from theirs might do more damage than good. And to be honest, his bear was driving him mad, constantly pacing and swiping at the air, trying to catch and savor the elusive, wavering scent of their mate.

This time when they went upstairs, Travis led Phoenix to his door instead of hers.

He captured her lips in a searing kiss, then murmured, "Come inside with me?"

*P*hoenix didn't even hesitate. "Yes."

Travis gave her no time to second-guess herself and immediately pulled her into his apartment, backed her against the door and kissed her again.

As waves of heat rippled through her, she wrapped her arms around his neck, pulled herself up and hitched her legs around his waist.

He took immediate advantage, sliding one hand to cup her bottom and grinding himself against her.

She threw back her head and whimpered.

He buried his face in her neck and carefully scraped his teeth along the sensitive flesh there.

Phoenix shivered and clutched at his shoulders. "Travis, please."

With a guttural sound of approval, he turned and strode down the hallway.

A moment later, he tumbled Phoenix onto his bed and followed her down. Gently smoothing her hair away from her face, he stared into her eyes and asked, "Are you okay with this?"

"Yes. Travis, please, yes." Phoenix practically writhed beneath him, the blood in her veins on fire for him.

He leaned over and buried his nose in her neck

again, inhaling deep. When he pulled back, she would swear his bear was looking back at her from feral eyes.

"My bear thinks you're his," he rumbled. "Ours."

Maybe those words should have freaked her out, but instead they made something deep inside relax. "What does that mean?"

"It means he thinks you're our mate. If we do this, whether it's true or not, whether you shift or not, whether you're human or not, you'll always be our mate. And we will never let you go. Be sure, Phoenix. Be very sure."

Phoenix closed her eyes, tears burning there, then opened them again. He was telling her that he would never walk away, that she would never be alone again. She lifted a hand and cupped his jaw.

He leaned his cheek into her caress.

"If we do this, Travis, you *and* your bear will be mine. I won't ever walk away and I won't ever let you go. You'll be stuck with *me* forever. *You* need to be certain as well."

His eyes flared bright and he lowered his head to hers, capturing her lips in a searing hot kiss.

---

11

*S*IDE EFFECT OF sex all night: cranky Phoenix.

Five o'clock came entirely too early after a long night of loving and no time in her dream space. It seemed every time she was just about to get there, Travis woke her in the most amazing and unexpected of ways. Which hey, she wasn't exactly complaining.

Except now she had to take orders, deliver breakfast and generally act like a patient, kind human being when all she felt like doing was ripping people's faces off. And she didn't even have an animal side!

Which really wasn't something she wanted to think about. Because every time she thought about maybe, probably, most certainly being one hundred percent human, she got depressed.

And crankier.

"Hey, Phoenix, I've got something for you," Karl called from the corner booth in the back.

It was the first time she'd ever seen the cougars and wolves sit together at the diner, which made her rather suspicious, considering this was an almost replica of the weird grouping they'd had at the bar the night before. And just like then, they were all staring at her.

"What is it?"

There was a strangely familiar sound and then a very recognizable scent reached her.

Karl pushed the can of tuna he'd apparently just opened toward her.

She stared at it.

Then looked at him.

What the hell? Was she supposed to take the tuna?

"Seriously, Karl?" Dan exclaimed. "How is that supposed to help?"

Karl shrugged. "I figured if she's a cat, she might shift."

"I told you she's not a feline," Cole said.

"She might be, you never know. She might be a breed we've never met before."

Dan groaned. "She'd still smell like a cat, you idiot."

"Are you sure?"

"Yes!" Cole and Dan both shouted.

"Because I brought this too, just in case." He pulled something out of his pocket and tossed it at Phoenix.

She caught it in reflex, stared a minute, then carefully set it on the table.

"Is that a cat toy?" Max asked.

"It's filled with catnip. It should totally work if she's a feline."

Even though both Dan and Cole had insisted she couldn't possibly be a cat just seconds before, they still stared at Phoenix as if they expected her to pounce on the ball at any moment.

She shook her head. "Can I get you boys anything? Or are you just going to continue wasting my time?"

"Go on." Max waved his hand at her. "We'll call you if we need anything."

As she walked away, a flurry of whispers occurred at her back.

"I was sure it would work!" Karl exclaimed.

"Not if she's not a cat!"

"It's not a bad idea, though. Hold on. I've got an idea!" A moment later, Pete rushed by and out the door.

Shaking her head, Phoenix continued to make her rounds, checking in with the customers, taking orders and delivering food and drinks.

When she made it back to the corner table the next time, Pete was back in his regular spot and had a huge grin on his face. "Here." He shoved a tiny bouquet of dandelions at her.

Phoenix reflexively caught the weeds in her hand and stared at them, then at Pete, then back down at the dandelions. What was she supposed to do with these?

"Do they make you hungry?" Pete asked eagerly.

"Gross," Dan exclaimed. "Why would they make her hungry?"

"I thought she might be a bunny," Pete said. "When my wolf goes hunting, he always checks the dandelion patches first because that's where all the rabbits go to eat."

Phoenix stared at him, then said dryly, "Well, I guess it's a good thing I'm not a bunny then."

Max snorted. "Sorry, Phoenix. I know my wolves are idiots, but they're just trying to help."

She nodded. "Right. Okay. Well. Can I get you guys anything else?"

"Nah, we're good."

"Great."

As she walked away this time, she heard Cole announce rather loudly that food was definitely not the way to go.

Rolling her eyes, she decided unless they flagged her down, she would ignore their table for the rest of her shift.

An hour later, the wolves and cougars were headed out the door and Phoenix was happily clearing their table. The rest of her shift passed uneventfully and soon enough, she was walking back into her apartment, pathetically grateful to be home. Without a second's pause, she crossed to the bed and collapsed.

A knock on the door roused her timeless minutes later. She glanced at the clock, but realized she hadn't looked at it when lying down so she had no idea how many minutes she'd been napping.

No idea.

This was terrible!

What if she'd only been asleep for forty-five minutes? Or *twenty*-five minutes? What if she'd slept for two hundred and ten minutes? She had no idea whether she should be cranky or celebrating. Happy and rested or depressed and tired.

Another knock came at the door.

Throwing off her blankets, she stomped over and flung it open.

"You!" She grabbed Travis by the shirt and pulled him into her apartment. "It's all your fault!"

Travis grinned at her. "What's wrong, darlin'?"

Why was he smiling?

"Don't you darlin' me! I had to deal with those wolves and cougars on zero minutes in my dream space and it's all your fault. And then, just now, I was napping, but I don't know how many minutes I was napping, now do I? And then you knocked and now I'm not napping. I'm not napping for any minutes, counted or not. I'm awake. And it's all your fault!"

~

Travis just couldn't help it. She was so flippin' adorable, stalking back and forth, waving her arms and ranting about naps and minutes and who knew what else.

He grabbed her up and kissed her breathless.

Of course, she kissed him back, which just sealed her fate.

He lifted her high and carried her over to the bed and they broke it in just like they'd broken his in the night before.

And just like then, it was amazing.

"What time is it?" Phoenix murmured. She was curled into him, her head resting on his chest, one leg slung over his.

"3:15."

"4:15 – 60, 4:45 – 90, 5:00 – 105," she murmured. "One hundred and five glorious minutes. I will kill you if you wake me before 5:00, Travis."

He couldn't help but grin. "All right, darlin'."

"I'm serious, Travis. One hundred and five minutes. No less."

"I promise."

He hadn't expected this. Whatever it was. This amazing feeling, this sense of protectiveness, of being so completely enamored of another person. Was this what it was like to have a mate?

If she finally shifted and they weren't true mates, it would break his heart. His bear's too.

But no.

There was no way she was anything other than their mate. He knew it. And his bear knew it too. Even if she never shifted, even if she did shift and the true mate bond never happened, he and his bear were in agreement.

She was theirs.

And so he lay there.

Unexpectedly content to simply hold his beautiful Phoenix in his arms.

To play with her hair and listen to her soft breathing.

To know that she'd gone someplace she called her dream space and that she was happy to visit there while sleeping in his arms.

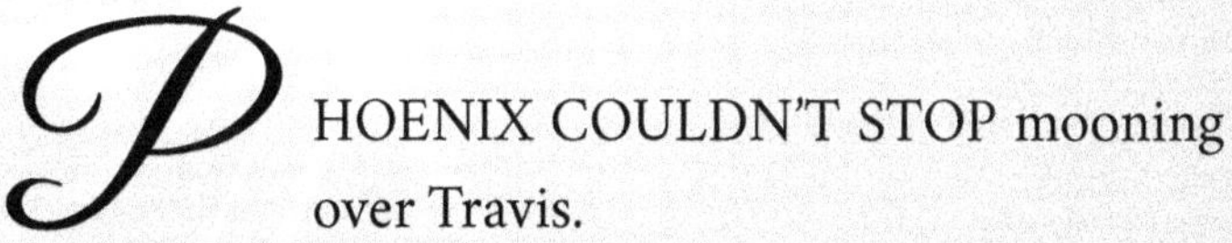

12

PHOENIX COULDN'T STOP mooning over Travis.

He'd actually let her sleep. For the full one hundred and five minutes.

Actually he'd let her sleep an additional ten.

Just because.

One hundred and fifteen glorious minutes, all of them spent curled up in his arms, warm and safe in her dream space like always, but *also* warm and safe in the real world.

She was simply so in love with him.

She had no idea how it had happened. How this amazing man with a black bear inside him had become so important to her happiness.

Not too long ago, she hadn't even known shifters

existed and now she was in love with a black bear shifter, claiming him as her mate.

And completely over the moon about it.

About him.

Her mate who was currently leaning over the bar, chatting with one of the wolves. His dark hair was all mussed up, hanging in his eyes and as she watched, he threw back his head and laughed at something the wolf said.

So freaking sexy.

"Hey, Phoenix, you ever gonna deliver those beers you got there?" one of the wolves called.

Damnit. She'd zoned out again.

She blamed the bear. It was all his fault. "Damn sexy bear," she muttered as she stomped over to the wolves' table.

Just as she reached them, something grabbed her by the ankles.

She shrieked and all the beers went flying. She glared at her feet where one of the cougars had his paws wrapped around her ankles.

Seconds later, Travis was at her side and if she thought she was pissed, she'd never seen that look in his eyes before.

The cougar obviously thought so too because suddenly her ankles were free and the cougar was shrinking back under the table where he'd obviously been napping moments before.

"Are you okay?" Travis asked her.

She nodded. "He just startled me that's all."

Travis stared at her a few moments, then slowly leaned over, glared under the table and let loose a hugely terrifying bear roar.

The cougar whimpered and didn't move.

"Don't touch her again!" Travis snarled.

Straightening, he pulled her close, kissed her fiercely, then released her and stalked back to the bar.

Swallowing, Phoenix glanced at the wolves, then under the table at the cougar. "Sorry about that. I'll go grab you guys some more beers."

~

Max waited until Phoenix was out of earshot, then pounded his fist on the table. "Get out from under there, you mangy cat." Just like he'd predicted. Out of hand. Fast.

Cole slid from under the table and slowly stretched to his full height, seamlessly flowing from cougar to man. Grabbing the shirt he'd left on the back of his chair, he pulled it on, then his jeans. "I can't believe that didn't work," he muttered.

"Well, it sort of worked," Pete said. "She was definitely startled."

"Yeah, but not really scared," Dan said.

"He's right." Cole jerked out his chair and slumped into it. "I didn't scent any fear at all. What kind of shifter isn't scared of a cougar?"

"What kind of *woman* isn't scared when her ankles are grabbed?" Pete countered.

They all stared over at the bar where Travis had Phoenix wrapped in his arms.

"That right there's why it didn't work," Karl said, pointing at the two of them.

"What do you mean?" Dan asked.

"She's got a bear protecting her. Of course she wasn't scared!"

Max grunted. "You're lucky you didn't get mauled, Cole."

"True, but it was worth it." Cole said.

"How do you figure?" Pete asked.

"Because now we know exactly what we need to do next."

Max was almost afraid to ask. "And what's that exactly?"

"Get rid of the bear, of course."

Like he'd said. Completely out of hand.

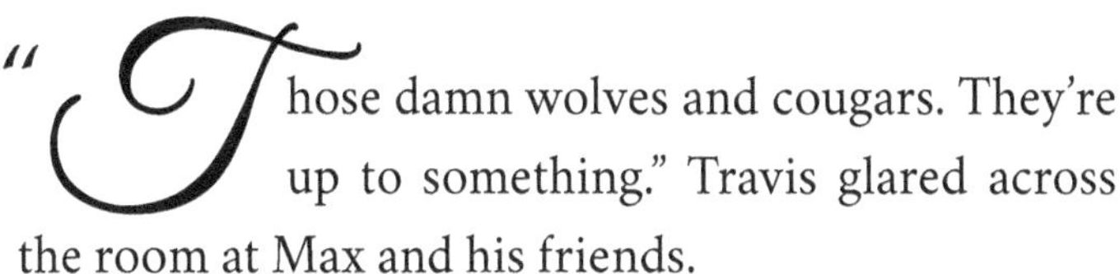

"Those damn wolves and cougars. They're up to something." Travis glared across the room at Max and his friends.

Phoenix smiled, completely charmed at his growly protectiveness. "Hey, don't worry about them." She stood on her tiptoes, cupped his cheeks and landed a kiss on his jaw. "They're harmless."

He shifted his gaze to her. "Harmless, huh?"

"Completely." She leaned up and kissed him again, this time on his lips.

He wrapped an arm around her waist and pulled her tight against him, capturing her lips with his.

Waves of heat washed over Phoenix as all thoughts of the wolves and cougars and whatever they might be up to were blown away by his kiss.

Long minutes later, he finally set her back on her feet and then steadied her when she swayed a bit.

"It's like I'm the only one working tonight," Cassie teased from the other side of the bar.

Phoenix laughed. "Sorry, Cassie. I'll stop distracting him."

She spun out of his reach, grabbed up her tray of

beers and hurried around the counter. As she walked away, she heard Cassie tell Travis that she needed a round of The Beast Within.

Phoenix groaned.

She'd only ever served The Beast Within once. Travis didn't even keep the bottle with his regular stock because he claimed it was best served sparingly. The alcohol's claim to be "so potent it'll bring your beast out" had turned out to be surprisingly accurate, as she'd witnessed her first night in the bar during what she now referred to as The Furbrawl.

She wasn't exactly looking forward to a repeat occurrence.

Glancing over her shoulder, she saw that Travis had disappeared, probably gone into the back to fetch the bottle.

Great.

Another brawl coming up.

She turned back around and froze. A giant wolf stood on the table directly in front of her, fangs bared, a low growl emanating from his throat.

Movement to her right and left made her realize there were wolves and cougars pacing on either side of her.

"Seriously?" A quick glance told her that Max's table was now empty, which meant these yahoos were still messing with her. "You do realize you can't drink your beers in animal form, right?" She stalked past the wolf and delivered their beers to their table as if they were still sitting there.

Turning around, she saw they had all followed her and now surrounded her again. Truthfully, it kind of freaked her out, but she wasn't about to show them any fear. "I'd shift back if I were you. You're still paying for these beers even if they get warm."

She stalked forward and to her relief, they parted to let her pass. She reached the bar at the same time Travis did.

"How many, Cassie?" he asked.

"Five."

He groaned. "Please don't tell me it's for Max and his crew."

"Sorry." She grinned.

"I thought Phoenix was serving them tonight."

Cassie nodded, then leaned forward. "I think they didn't want her to freak out. You know—because of what happened last time."

"That's ridiculous," Phoenix said. "I'm not going to freak out."

"Of course not," Travis said. "Here." He set the five shot glasses on her tray. "You can deliver them since Cassie's got her hands full with the party room. But you tell them I said they're paying for any damages and they'd better not lay a hand on you."

Phoenix rolled her eyes. "I'll let them know." She picked up the tray and headed back over to what she now referred to as The Crazy Table.

"Five shots of The Beast Within." She handed them out and started to turn away.

"Holy shit!" Pete exclaimed.

She swung back around. "What?"

"That's it! We need another shot."

"What?"

"We need one more shot. Go ask Travis for another shot."

Phoenix huffed. "Fine." She went up to the bar, collected another shot from Travis and took it back to their table. "Here you go." She set it down and started to turn away.

"No, wait!" Karl said.

"You have to drink with us," Dan said.

"What? Why? No. It doesn't matter why. I can't. I'm working."

"But you have to," Pete said. "This stuff always works. Always. It wakes the beast within and brings him out. It'll work on you. Come on. Drink with us."

Phoenix really didn't like this plan at all. She

didn't want to unleash her beast in the middle of the bar. But even more, she didn't want to NOT unleash her beast in the middle of the bar.

She stared at the shot glass that sat on the table. If Pete was right and it always released the inner animal, this would be the proof she needed.

This was her answer.

Shifter or not.

Human or not.

She glanced over her shoulder at Travis.

If she didn't shift, would she lose him?

And if so, wasn't it better to know now? Now before she fell even deeper in love. Before there was no recovering from the heartache of his rejection?

Taking a deep breath, she picked up the shot glass.

"Bottoms up!" She downed it in one quick gulp, a scalding, liquid fire that spread through her veins and lit her from the inside out. Seriously. If she had a beast, it would be roaring right about now.

As she lifted her watery eyes to the rest of the table, she saw none of them had drunk theirs. "Aren't you going to drink?"

"Sure. In a minute," Cole said.

"How are you feeling?" Pete asked.

She shrugged. "Fine." But not really. Suddenly she

was so freaking sleepy. "I need a nap," she muttered. All that fire had drained her energy away.

"It should have happened by now," Karl said.

"Well, we don't know what kind of animal she is, so it might take longer," Max said.

"What's the longest it's ever taken?" Pete asked.

"Longest I heard was a minute and thirty seconds," Karl said, "but I think that's just an urban legend."

"Yeah, that's impossible," Dan said.

"Well, how long's it been?" Karl asked.

"Not sure. Maybe a minute," Cole said.

All of these words seemed to come from a faraway place. She heard them, but it was like they were coming at her through water. "I need to lie down." She turned away and slowly walked, one foot in front of the other, toward the bar.

"Hey, are you okay?" Travis suddenly appeared at her side.

"I'm suddenly not feeling well," Phoenix said, trying to carefully enunciate her words, not wanting Travis to know that she'd just gotten drunk off one shot of The Beast Within.

Drunk.

Not shifted. Just drunk.

She was definitely human.

She suddenly wanted to cry as much as she wanted to sleep. She was so desperate for sleep. "I'm going upstairs. I'm sorry."

"No, it's okay. Do you need help?"

"No. I'm fine. I'll see you later." Phoenix carefully walked the length of the bar, turned left and headed down the hall toward the bathrooms and stairs. Everything looked so weird. The walls seemed to bulge and waver before her eyes. She made it to the stairs and slowly, one foot at a time climbed them. When she reached the top, she staggered down the hall.

It took her three tries to get the door open, but then she was inside.

She carefully closed the door behind her, walked into the bedroom and crawled onto Travis' bed. His scent barreled over her and she collapsed.

The dream space that she always slid into so carefully, quietly and easily, roared over her in a violent wave of sound, the drumming a loud beat that kept time to the rush of blood in her veins and the fire that would not die.

13

THE MINUTE PHOENIX disappeared, Travis headed straight for Max's table.

"What did you idiots do to Phoenix?" he growled, noting that five of the six shots he'd poured were still sitting on the table untouched.

The cougars and wolves exchanged uneasy glances.

"Well?"

"It should have worked," Pete said sullenly.

"I agree," Max said. "This isn't exactly good news."

"What should have worked?" Travis asked.

"The sixth shot was for her." Karl nodded at the empty glass. "She downed it fast, but then nothing happened."

"Shit," Travis growled. "Are you telling me she just did a shot of The Beast Within?"

"Yeah, but nothing happened!" Karl said.

Travis spun around and scanned the room. The minute he saw Glory, he headed her way. "I need you to take over the bar."

"What? Why?"

"I've gotta check on Phoenix."

Glory scanned the bar. "Where is she?"

"Just watch the bar," Travis growled and stormed away.

~

"You did *what*?"

Max winced. He wouldn't want to be Pete right now.

Glory looked like she might claw off his face at any moment. "We have no idea what kind of shifter she is and you thought ripping her animal free with The Beast Within was a good idea?"

Pete shrugged. "Well… yeah."

"It should have worked," Karl insisted.

"I've never seen a shifter restrain their animal after a shot of The Beast," Dan said.

"He's right." Max shook his head. "Which means this is more serious than we thought."

Glory huffed. "You didn't see any evidence of a shift at all? No claws, no fur or feathers, nothing?"

"Nothing."

"I've gotta go watch the bar, but you boys better be on your best behavior. You take those shots, you control your beasts. Got me?"

Max and his crew all nodded.

"Don't worry about us, Glory," Pete said. "We're going to do a bit more planning before we have these here shots."

"Yeah, we gotta figure out our next steps," Cole said.

Max just rolled his eyes and wondered how much worse things could get.

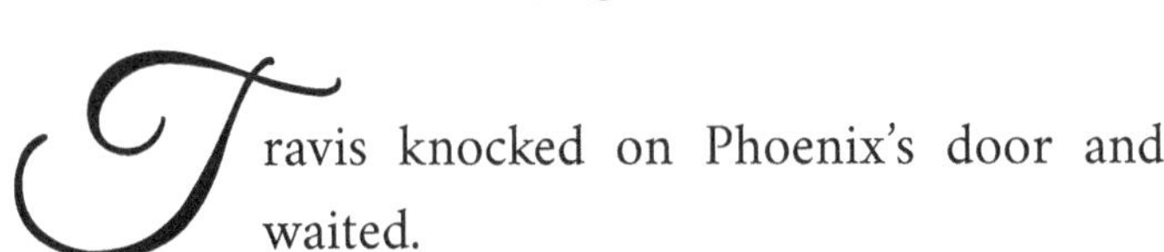

Travis knocked on Phoenix's door and waited.

There was no answer.

Remembering how unhappy she'd been the last time he woke her from her nap, he opened the door quietly, but realized almost immediately she wasn't there.

Closing the door, he crossed the hall, entered his own apartment and headed for the bedroom.

At the center of his bed, Phoenix rested, curled in a small ball, bathed in a pool of moonlight.

He'd never felt the intensity of tenderness and joy that welled inside at the sight of her. She was so beautiful and peaceful. And she was in his bed.

All he wanted to do was crawl in beside her.

Even though he and his bear had both hoped to find her in shifted form, he wasn't even disappointed. And neither, he realized, was his bear. They were both simply too charmed and enchanted by the sight of Phoenix in their bed, sleeping peacefully in the middle of their territory.

Glory could handle the bar.

He was going to take a nap with his mate.

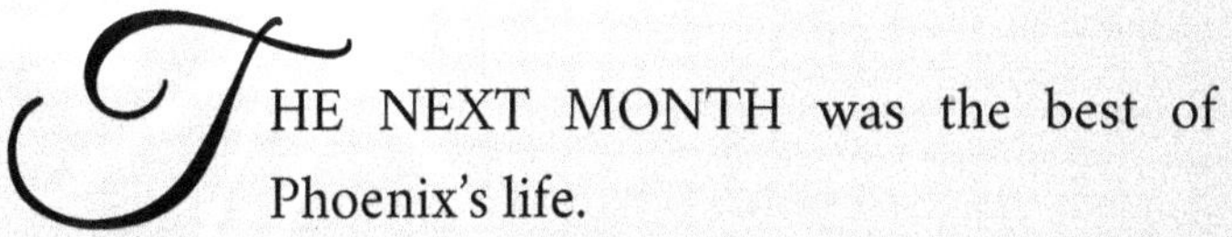

THE NEXT MONTH was the best of Phoenix's life.

Travis started dropping into the diner each morning for a late breakfast. He'd always sit in her section and tease her with kisses each time she stopped at his table. He usually timed it so that she was just about to get off work. He'd order breakfast for both of them and then when her shift ended, she'd join him and they'd eat together.

Then, she'd follow him back to the bar, where he'd work in his office while she took a nap. No matter what time she woke, though, whether it was forty-five minutes or one hundred and twenty minutes later, he'd always be curled around her, holding her snug to his chest, face buried in her hair.

After long and lazy minutes lying in each other's arms, kissing and cuddling and indulging their passion, they'd get up, have dinner together and work in the bar side-by-side.

And at the end of each night, they'd go back upstairs and lose themselves in each other once again. Sometimes the loving was slow and sweet and sometimes it was frantic and rough. But always, *always*, it was amazing. And then they'd fall asleep. And later, much later, she'd wake in his arms, the steady beat of his heart echoing the drum from her dream.

And the best part of it all?

No matter what time of the day, no matter how busy Travis was, no matter whether it was a short nap or a long one, *she never woke alone.*

It made her chest tight to think about. That after so many years of endless wandering, she might have finally found what she hadn't even known she was looking for.

The only downside was that she still hadn't shifted. All the efforts of the wolves and cougars hadn't resulted in anything.

At first, she'd been upset, but the more time that passed and the more Travis' attitude toward her didn't change, the more she realized he really didn't care.

He wanted to be with her, no matter whether she had an animal inside or not. And that was enough for her.

Of course, the wolves and cougars weren't exactly giving up.

In fact, they now had a huge betting pool going. They had bets on everything: on when and where she'd first shift, on what or who would cause the first shift and on what animal she'd shift into.

Most of the money was on Travis. That somehow his black bear would pull her animal out.

Some of the bets were disturbing though.

There was a lot of money on fear being the impetus for her to change, which didn't make her happy at all.

Of course, when Phoenix found out about the betting pool, she decided to place her own bets.

Fifty bucks on never and another fifty on human.

Everyone protested.

"How do you win a never bet?" Karl demanded.

"And there's no way you're human, Phoenix," Pete said. "We've told you a thousand times. You don't smell human."

"Fine." Phoenix stomped up to the board, drew a slash after human and wrote the word latent.

Human / Latent

Silence fell for a moment, then Max said, "Well, if it's true, that's okay, Phoenix. You're one of us now."

Phoenix had to blink back tears at that statement and at the chorus of agreements that followed.

"Still. How do you win a never bet?" Karl asked again.

"I guess we need a time limit," Pete said. "Otherwise, the money might sit in the pool forever."

"Yeah, but that'd be like we gave up," Cole protested. "We're not giving up on Phoenix, not ever."

Jeez. She was going to bawl like a baby if they didn't stop.

"How about an ongoing pool?" Max said. "We can set an initial time limit of ninety days and if Phoenix is still unshifted at that time, she wins the pool. Then we'll just start a new one for a new round of ninety days."

Phoenix thought this was a terrible idea. It sounded like the men were going to be betting on her shifter status for the rest of her life.

Of course, Travis loved the idea because the bar got a percentage of the take.

As soon as the wolves and cougars realized they only had ninety days to win the money already in the pool, they immediately intensified their efforts to force Phoenix to shift.

Which meant they were back on their scare Phoenix campaign.

It was beginning to feel a lot like the lottery of her life.

"I just don't understand," Cole said glumly. "She didn't even scream when she saw the snake."

Max snorted. Not only had Phoenix not screamed, she'd actually carried the snake out to the woods where she'd released him.

"Why on earth would she scream?" Glory asked. "It was just a snake, and not a very big one at that."

"I would have screamed," Pete said.

"See?" Cole waved an arm at him. "Perfectly normal reaction to unexpectedly having a snake drop on a table you're cleaning."

"I get not being afraid of snakes," Dan said. "Not

everyone is. But what animal isn't afraid when surrounded by cougars and wolves?"

They all turned and stared at Phoenix.

"She's even tamed Travis and that bear's intimidating," Pete said.

Max snorted at the same time Glory did.

Their eyes met for a brief moment, before she jerked hers away. "Well, I gotta say you guys aren't going to be winning this bet anytime soon." She stood and walked away.

"I'm thinking maybe I should change my bet," Cole said, "since I'm beginning to doubt my unicorn theory."

"Oh, you're just *now* beginning to doubt it?" Max said dryly.

"Yeah, because I'm pretty sure a unicorn would be thoroughly intimidated by that bear, not to mention all the wolves and cougars in this room right now."

"Well, I'm not changing my bet," Pete said.

Max wasn't surprised. Pete was still convinced that eventually Phoenix would explode into a mythical bird and prove him right.

"I might make a new bet though. I'm thinking if she's not a phoenix, she might be a snake."

Everyone stared at him.

"Well, she wouldn't be intimidated by them if she is one, right?"

"Good point," Dan said. "But even if she is, how do we get her to shift?"

The question of the hour.

Max didn't want to admit it, but he was starting to think that maybe Phoenix was right and she *was* latent. She definitely wasn't human, but growing up without any shifters around may have permanently affected the development of her shifter side.

At least it didn't appear to be as big an issue as they'd feared.

Glory was still concerned, but Max was pretty certain that Travis would be okay no matter what happened. He clearly adored Phoenix and his bear seemed happy too.

"You know what every animal's afraid of?" Pete suddenly said.

Max wasn't sure he even wanted to know what Pete was thinking at the moment, but before he could discourage him from sharing, Cole asked, "What?"

"Fire."

"Hell, no," Max exclaimed.

"Are you crazy?" Karl asked. "Travis would kill us if we burned down his bar!"

"Yeah, but not before Glory castrated us all," Cole said.

Max winced along with the others.

"Well, I'm out of ideas," Pete said.

"Yeah, me too," Dan muttered.

The rest of the men reluctantly agreed.

Max just shook his head. It would be a true tragedy if Phoenix ended up winning the betting pool after all.

15

"YOU OKAY, DARLIN'?" Travis caught Phoenix behind the neck and pulled her over the bar for a steamy kiss.

Long minutes later, she pulled away and murmured, "Yeah, I'm fine."

"Max's crew still giving you a hard time?" Travis threw a glare over her shoulder. Those stupid mutts and alley cats needed to stop harassing his mate.

She shrugged. "I can handle it. I know they're just trying to help."

"Did you see their faces when she carried that snake out of here?" A rasping cough preceded Cassie as she stepped up to the bar.

"Jeez, you sound terrible, Cassie!" Phoenix exclaimed.

Cassie waved a hand airily. "It's just a cold. I'll be fine."

"Wait. Shifters get colds?"

Travis grinned at the stunned look on Phoenix's face. "Of course we do since there's still no cure for the common cold."

"Well, sure, but I thought maybe–"

The rattling sound of Cassie's laugh made Phoenix cringe. "You've been watching too many Hollywood movies. Or maybe reading too many steamy romances."

Travis grinned at the blush on Phoenix's face. When did she have time to read? All the woman ever seemed to do was work, eat and sleep. And play sexy games with him, of course.

"You should go home, Cassie," Phoenix said. "Glory and I can handle the rest of the night. You should get some rest."

"She's right," Travis said.

"I'm fine. There's only an hour left. I just need–" she leaned over the bar and rooted around on the shelf beneath it. "Aha!" She popped up and grinned at them. "I knew I left my cough drops here last night."

What occurred next happened so quickly Travis could never get it straight in his head – what happened first, what happened next.

Everything just seemed to happen all at once.

Cassie opened her bag of cough drops and several flew through the air.

A brown blur flashed by on the bar, Cassie screamed and then her bag of cough drops were gone and so was Phoenix.

Travis panicked and swung around, but didn't see her anywhere.

"I don't believe it," Cassie exclaimed. She was staring up above his head.

Travis looked up, but didn't see anything. He swung around and realized the entire bar had come to a standstill.

Everyone was on their feet and they were all staring at a point high above his head.

Travis hurried around the bar and looked up.

Deep in the shadows at the very top of the bar, he could barely make out movement. "What is she? Did anyone see her animal?"

"She was brown," Cassie said. "That's all I really saw."

"How in the world did she even get up there?" The ledge Phoenix was sitting on was only about a foot below the ceiling.

"Climbed the wall," Max said.

"And man, was she fast," Cole said.

"Here." Glory shoved her way through and handed Travis the ladder they used to change the lightbulbs. "See if you can coax her down."

Travis went back behind the bar, set up the ladder and began to climb. As he got closer to her hiding spot, he crooned to her, "Hey, darlin', it's okay. It's just me. I'm so happy you finally came out to play."

When he reached the top of the bar and finally saw his mate's shifted form for the first time, Travis' heart just about melted in his chest, she was that cute. Big nose. Dark, round eyes. Brown fur. White chest. Big ears with white tufts of fur sticking out of them.

She stared at him from her spot just out of arm's reach.

"You are so flippin' adorable. Come here, sweetheart."

She hesitated, then slowly inched toward him, Cassie's bag of cough drops gripped tight in the tiny black claws of her front paws.

"That's right, darlin', come here." He held out his arms and she leapt into them, her arms and legs latching onto his shirt. She curled into him, much the same way he'd seen her curl into their bed for a nap. He wrapped his left arm around her, anchoring her small form to his chest, and slowly backed his way down the ladder.

When he turned to face his sister and their friends, everyone gasped.

"She's so cute!" Cassie exclaimed. "She's like a little teddy bear."

"What is she?" Pete asked. "I've never seen such a tiny bear before."

"I don't think she's a bear," Travis said. "I think she's a koala."

"But aren't koalas bears?" Cassie asked.

"Yeah," Karl said, "Koala bears."

Travis shook his head. "I don't think they're bears. She doesn't smell like a bear."

"She's a marsupial," Glory announced, staring down at her phone.

"A mar–what?" Pete asked.

"A marsupial. They have pouches where they carry their babies, just like kangaroos."

"But that means she's Australian!" Karl said. "She doesn't sound Australian."

"That's because she grew up here," Travis said.

"Can we pet her?" Karl asked.

"Yeah, bring her around the bar, Travis. Stop hogging her!" Pete said.

Travis rolled his eyes, but after checking Phoenix's expression to make sure she wasn't too freaked out – she had her face turned toward their friends and was just watching them – he walked around the bar.

"She's just adorable," Glory said, reaching out a tentative hand to stroke Phoenix's back.

Travis made a slow circuit around the bar, allowing each of their friends to gently pet Phoenix and murmur their congratulations to her.

"What's she holding onto?" Dan asked when Travis reached him.

"My cough drops!" Cassie stepped forward to take the bag from Phoenix, but Phoenix pulled the bag closer to her body and let out a strange yipping, squeaking sound.

It reminded Travis of the squeaky dog toy Cole had given Max for his birthday last year.

Cassie chuckled. "Okay, you can keep them. I'll get some more later." She reached out a hand and gently scratched Phoenix's head. "You are just the cuddliest thing." She looked up at Travis. "You're so lucky. I want to go kidnap a real koala now."

Travis barked out a laugh. "I don't think Australia would appreciate that." He turned to Glory. "I'm going to take her upstairs now. Can you close down the bar tonight?"

"Of course. Go on." She shooed him away with her hands.

"Hey, Phoenix," Max called.

Travis turned so she could see his face.

"Welcome to life as a shifter. We're so very happy for you." He spread his arms as if to indicate everyone in the bar.

Travis nodded his thanks, turned and carried his mate upstairs.

~

"So who won the bet?" Pete asked.

"Glory?" Max turned and looked at her.

"Well…" Glory consulted their board. "It looks like Cole was the only one who had money on today, so he won that pool. No one guessed koala, so I don't know what we're supposed to do with that money. Let's see. I'm not really sure what caused her to shift. Any ideas?"

"She wanted my cough drops," Cassie said.

"That doesn't even make any sense," Karl

complained. "The tuna didn't work. The catnip didn't work."

"And the dandelions," Pete said. "Don't forget them."

"Right, tuna, catnip, dandelions. None of those worked, but cough drops did?"

"I guess koalas don't like those other things," Cassie said.

"But they like cough drops?" Cole asked incredulously.

"Not cough drops," Glory said, staring at her phone again. "Eucalyptus leaves."

Cassie giggled. "Okay, that makes sense."

"How so?" Dan asked.

"My cough drops have eucalyptus in them."

"Well, that's disappointing," Pete muttered.

"Very," Karl agreed. "I don't know how we could have guessed that."

16

TRAVIS CARRIED PHOENIX into his apartment and settled into his armchair with her still cuddled against him.

Once they were settled, he carefully lifted one paw and examined it. Her claws might be small, but they were thick and wicked looking. Probably good for climbing things like the bar or trees in the wild.

Her paws were padded and each had five distinct digits, three together and two off to the side.

"So you have two thumbs, eh?" He tucked her paw back against his chest and continued his explorations, stroking one hand up and down her back gently.

Her fur was thick and and fluffy, not as soft as he

expected, but more textured, reminding him of a sheep's wool.

Her ears were about the cutest things he'd ever seen. He could only access one at the moment because the other was resting against his chest, but she had little tufts of white sticking out, going every which way. He gently stroked a finger along the curve of her ear and chuckled when she made a small yipping sound and pulled away from his chest to stare up at him.

"Hey there, my sweet love." He leaned over and kissed her on her forehead, right above her leathery nose.

She blinked sleepily at him, then carefully walked herself down his shirt until she sat on his lap.

She looked around, then climbed off his lap, swung herself around so her hind legs dangled off the couch and walked herself down to the floor.

"Where are you going, darlin'?"

She looked up at him, then turned and ran across the room.

Travis couldn't believe how adorable she was.

She ran on all fours, kind of lunging forward with each step, her bottom doing this cute little wobble as she moved. At the door to the hallway, she stopped and looked back at him.

He grinned and stood. "Shall I follow you, yeah?"

She turned and ran down the hall and darted into his bedroom.

By the time Travis reached his doorway, she'd managed to climb onto the bed and sat in the middle, watching him and waiting.

"Ready for a nap, aren't you?" He stripped off his clothes and debated whether to shift. "What do you think, darlin'? Bear or human form?"

She just watched him expectantly, so he went ahead and shifted, landing on all four paws and freezing there, waiting to see if she would freak out.

Phoenix hopped to the end of the bed and stared at him for a long moment. She then hopped back to the middle, glancing back at him as if in invitation.

Travis huffed in pure joy and climbed onto the bed.

The moment he stretched out on his belly, Phoenix pulled herself up onto his back and settled there, back legs tucked under her, front legs sprawled across his massive shoulders, face settled into the hollow of his neck.

Travis' bear had never felt so settled or content in his life.

*P*hoenix was dreaming just like always.

The soft beat of a drum echoed and she stretched, moving slowly from one dream space – dark, safe and quiet – to another, still shaded, but lighter, with the scent of woods and of home all around her.

She was cradled in the soft embrace of a tree, right in the nook where branches and trunk met.

She looked up and saw her mate stretched on a limb high above.

He dropped one of his arms toward her and she reached for it.

He was too far away, so she climbed the trunk a ways, then reached again.

She caught hold of his paw, and he lifted her enough so she could grasp his shoulder and climb onto his back. She curled into his warm body, pressed her ear to his fur and listened as the beat of his heart lulled her back to sleep.

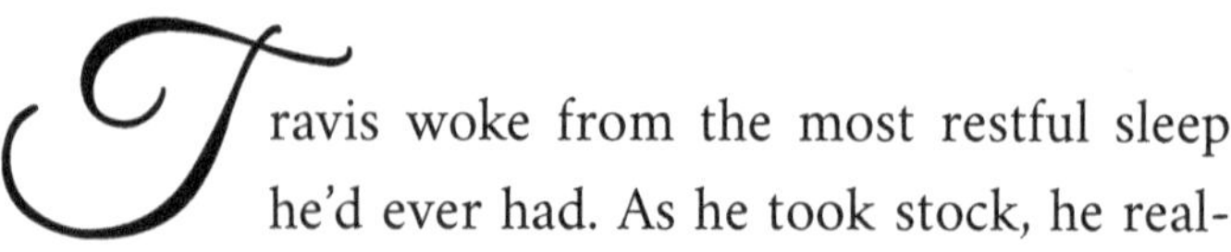

*T*ravis woke from the most restful sleep he'd ever had. As he took stock, he realized he was back in his human form, as was Phoenix, who was still sprawled on top of him.

He rolled to the side while carefully sliding her around so that she tipped off his back into his arms.

She curled into him, as adorably cuddly in human form as she'd been in her koala one.

"You were in my dreams," she murmured.

He smiled. "You were in mine too."

She stretched and opened her eyes to stare into his. "No one's ever been in my dream space before. Not ever. I've always been alone there. Lately though I kept dreaming there was something just out of reach, something I was longing for but couldn't quite get to. I never knew what it was, but then, today I did. It was you."

"It's like I told you, darlin'. We're mates. *True* mates." Just saying the words made his throat tighten in gratitude and his bear rumble joyfully, *Ours*.

"I shifted, didn't I?" Phoenix asked abruptly.

Travis smiled tenderly at her. "You certainly did."

"I was really small. A lot smaller than you."

"It stands to reason. You're a lot smaller than me in human form too."

Phoenix nodded. "Did I understand you right? I'm a koala?"

He nodded. "A freaking unbelievably adorable

koala. Seriously. I've never seen anything cuter in my life."

*P*hoenix relaxed at his statement. "You don't mind that I'm not a black bear like you?"

"I can't imagine you as anything other than the sweet koala you are." He leaned over and kissed her, gently at first, but then with greater passion as he swept his tongue inside and stole every thought she had.

Heat unfurled between them and she pressed closer, so completely enamored of this man, this black bear, who'd so unexpectedly come into her life, who was everything she'd never known she wanted.

17

"I STILL DON'T understand why she never shifted before now," Karl said in exasperation.

It was Sunday afternoon and although the bar was normally closed on Sundays, Travis had opened it and invited all their friends over to celebrate Phoenix's first shift.

"Especially after she had a shot of The Beast Within," Pete said. "It's never failed to pull the beast from any shifter I've ever known."

Travis grinned. "You want to enlighten them, darlin'?"

Phoenix had spent the entire morning researching koalas, trying to understand her animal side better. "Did you guys know that koalas in the wild sleep anywhere from 18 to 22 hours a day?"

"Wow. Really?" Glory asked.

Phoenix nodded. "Yep. And when I had that shot, well… the koala within decided it was time to take a nap. Right. Then. I barely made it upstairs in time. I've never been so tired in my entire life. And I love to nap."

"She really does," Travis said.

"Travis once mentioned to me that he thought my animal might be napping. I think he was right. I think she was napping all this time and never really came fully awake until she met Travis and his bear. Until she met all of you."

"So is she sleeping now?" Max asked.

Phoenix thought a minute, then nodded. "I think so. She's not awake very often. And when she is awake–" She stopped, not wanting to share the fact that her koala didn't really care about socializing with friends. All the koala wanted to do was curl into Travis. Whether he was in bear form or human form didn't really matter. Her koala simply loved their man-bear, just like Phoenix did.

"When she's awake what?" Pete asked.

"She's all mine," Travis said, tipping Phoenix's chin up and kissing her breathless.

Keep reading for an excerpt from Cole's story in
Witchy Shenanigans.

"They're back," Max announced.

Cole groaned and signaled Phoenix for another beer. He knew exactly what was coming and was pathetically grateful they were having their meeting at the local shifter bar, Shenanigans.

"Someone's gotta do something," Karl said. "We can't have humans just wandering through the woods. They could see anything!"

Max nodded. "Time to step up to the plate, Cole."

"Why me?" Cole demanded, even though he knew exactly what they were going to say.

"Because they're trespassing on cougar, not wolf, territory," Max said, "which means you've been nominated."

"Why not Dan? He's a cougar too!"

"You're crazy if you think I'm going to go talk to some human females about anything," Dan retorted.

"And what's wrong with human females?"

Everyone looked up at the question.

Phoenix stood there, a tray of beers in her hands and an annoyed look on her face.

Cole was relieved he wasn't the one she was glaring at. Phoenix had been raised among humans, so who knew what she'd do with Dan's beer now that he'd gotten her riled up?

Dan shrugged. "I suppose normal human females are okay, but these women – they're not normal."

"And how do you know that?"

Max cleared his throat. "Well, they keep trespassing on our lands while naked."

Phoenix stared at them for a long minute before finally asking, "Are you sure they're not shifters? Because my experience with humans is they're kind of prudish when it comes to nudity. Whereas y'all, meaning you shifters—"

"Uh, you're a shifter too," Dan interjected.

Cole winced. While that might be true, Phoenix had only recently discovered her shifter form and still considered herself to be more human than not, so he wasn't sure Dan's statement was going to help matters at all.

"*You* shifters," Phoenix repeated, raising her voice and ignoring Dan's statement, "tend to get naked at the drop of a hat. And not for any sexy shenanigans either, just for—"

"Oh, we get naked for sexy shenanigans too," Cole assured her.

She rolled her eyes. "Anyway, as I was saying, being naked in the woods tends to be a pretty big indicator of shifterhood."

Max sighed. "But they're not shifting, Phoenix. They smell human and all they do is walk into the woods buck naked, dance around in a circle, pick a few weeds and walk out again. Still naked."

"Interesting," Phoenix said. "Though I'm still not sure why it's a problem, even if it is unusual."

"They could see anything out there, Phoenix," Pete exclaimed. "That's where we shift. That's where the cubs run and play. And now we've got naked humans wandering around who might see something they shouldn't."

Cole sighed. "I'll go and talk to them."

"Excellent!" Max grinned. "Glad that's taken care of."

Cole grunted. Of course the damn wolf was happy. He wasn't the one who'd be dealing with crazy females, and human ones at that.

"What have you two done now?" Megan stalked inside The House of Light, the store she owned with her two sisters, and glared at them.

Lara and Jessica glanced at each other, then faced Megan together, looks of confused innocence on their faces, not that Megan bought that for a minute.

"What are you talking about, Megan?" Lara asked innocently.

"Oh and I suppose you two idiots have no idea why both Jerry and Steve just hit on me."

"Who're Jerry and Steve?" Jessica looked at Lara, who shrugged and said, "More importantly, are they cute?" Both women turned back to Megan expectantly.

"Cute?" Megan threw up her hands. "Maybe. If you consider ninety-eight-year-old men cute. You know how I know they're ninety-eight? Because they told me so. I learned their entire life stories in the five minutes they detained me outside C's. Steve went on and on about his stamina being great for his almost ten decades on earth and Jerry told me he'd rock my world if I'd only give him a chance. When the two started arguing about who would be a better match for me, I escaped into the store."

"Wait." Lara laughed. "Are you talking about those two old geezers who sit at that picnic table outside the grocery store all day long, chatting and playing chess?"

"Now you're getting it."

"Why, those old coots," Jessica said. "I had no idea they had it in them."

"I'm sure they don't. So why don't you two fess up? What have you been up to? Because it wasn't just Steve and Jerry."

"It wasn't?" Jessica grinned. "Well, come on. Who else was hitting on you?"

"Let's see, Craig Miller – you know, the married owner of C's – hit on me in the frozen foods section and then his daughter Barb asked me out when I was paying for my groceries."

"Isn't Barb engaged?" Lara asked.

"No, that's his other daughter, Natalie. But that's not the point! Why has everyone gone mad? Did you two cast another spell?"

Silence.

Megan stared at her sisters' guilty expressions. "You did, didn't you? What did you do this time?"

"It was only a little spell!" Lara burst out.

"We hardly gave it any power at all," Jessica said. "Just a little push, nothing major."

Megan huffed. "Your nothing major always turns into a disaster. I'd hate to see what you'd accomplish when you're really trying. Now tell me exactly what you did."

"We just burned some herbs and asked for help, that's all," Lara said.

"What herbs and help from whom?"

"Basil, nutmeg, bay leaves." Jessica said.

"Lavender, cinnamon," Lara said.

"Verbena, crocus," Jessica continued.

"Seriously? What'd you guys do? Use every herb associated with love potions?"

"Every one we had or could find." Jessica grinned.

"And that was a lot," Lara said. "Though we might need to replenish some of our stock."

Megan huffed out a breath. "And the help?"

"Eros and Aphrodite," Lara admitted.

"What is wrong with you two?" Megan exploded. "You just threw everything at the universe in the hopes of what? That chaos wouldn't come knocking?"

"Well, actually, we were just hoping for a virile, hot guy," Jessica said.

"Preferably one young enough to wear you out,"

Lara said. "We weren't exactly going for the nonagenarian set."

"Nona-what?" Jessica asked. "You just made that word up."

"I did not. It means someone who's in their 90s. I think at the very least the universe could have given Megan a sexagenarian."

Jessica laughed. "Yeah. A sexa-something anyway."

"You two are too much. You need to figure out how to reverse that spell and now. I don't have time for a man, even if he is a nonagenarian."

"I think we can do better than Jerry and Steve," Jessica said.

"Definitely," Lara agreed. "Maybe we need more lavender."

"Or elder. We really should have waited for our next order to come in," Jessica said.

"Or maybe not gone casting at all," Megan snapped.

"Oh, that wasn't an option," Lara said. "You're so uptight all the time, Megan. You're constantly working and driving us crazy, wanting us to do the same."

"And there it is," Megan said. "So you didn't even cast a love spell for my benefit."

"Of course it was for your benefit," Jessica said. "We're not the ones in dire need of sex."

"Ahem."

The cleared throat made all three women jump.

Megan whirled and gaped at the man standing just inside their shop door.

Tall and lean, with sandy-brown hair and green eyes, he was the epitome of the virile, hot guy Jessica had mentioned only moments before.

"Well, hello there," Lara said. "Can we help you?"

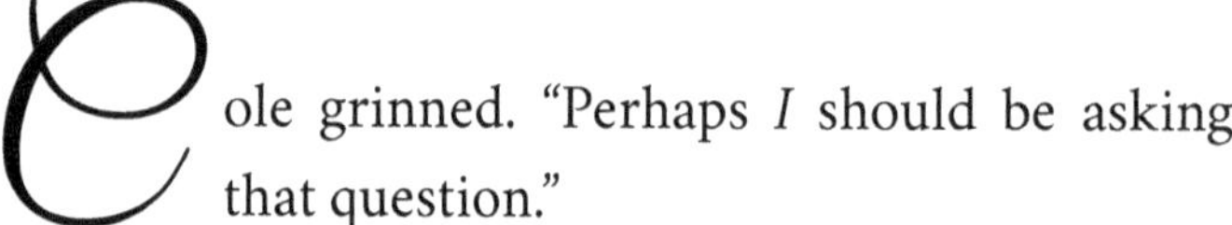

ole grinned. "Perhaps *I* should be asking that question."

Two of the women laughed, but the third glared daggers at him, even as a blush covered her face and traveled south. He wondered how far that blush went.

Ah, redheads. They were so much fun.

"Was there something you needed?" The angry blusher asked. "Because if not, we're very busy."

Cole made a show of glancing around the shop and then back her way. "Yes," he said dryly. "I can see that."

He didn't think it was possible, but her face turned even redder.

"So," one of the other women spoke brightly. "What brings you into our shop today? Were you looking for a gift, just window shopping or…" She let her words trail away suggestively.

Now Cole was in a quandary. He'd come here for a reason and had even rehearsed what he was going to say on the way over. How to say it without causing offense or suspicion. Now though, every word he'd rehearsed was gone from his head. Which wasn't necessarily a bad thing since accusing someone of trespassing was no way to make friends.

And he and his cat definitely wanted to make friends with these lovely ladies. In fact, the second he'd stepped into the store, his cougar, usually a lazy cat in the afternoons, had stretched and come to attention. His focus hadn't wavered from the three women in front of them since.

Closer, his cat rumbled.

With a sigh, Cole obliged and took a step forward, inhaling deeply. Their scents were different than he expected.

Human, but with something a bit more. A tang or a spice and one scent–

Ours. His cat swiped at the air, trying to catch that scent.

They're human, Cole snapped while fighting to keep claws and fur from sprouting. Stupid cat.

Ours.

Ugh.

The angry blusher made an exasperated sound and muttered something about defective spells as she swept behind the counter.

Great. He was off to a fabulous start.

"Don't mind her," one of the women said. "She's always like that."

"Cranky," the other woman agreed. "I'm Jessica and this is Lara."

Cole grinned and introduced himself, then asked if they were sisters.

"How could you tell?" Lara asked.

Cole laughed. "Just a wild guess." Involving lots of gorgeous red hair and freckles.

Not ours.

Of course they're not. I told you. They're human.

"Lara, Jessica," the woman behind the counter snapped. "We have work to do. If you're not going to help, you might as well just take off. And work on reversing something important."

Ours.

Jeez, his cat was ridiculous today.

Lara and Jessica both grinned.

"But Megan, I think it's working perfectly," Lara said.

"Yes," Jessica agreed, "I'm pretty sure we ordered hot and vir–"

"That's enough!" Megan snapped.

Megan, Cole's cat rumbled. *Closer.*

Cole obliged, moving across the room toward the counter where Megan was pretending to work. At least he thought she was pretending.

Ours. His cougar was now pressing against his skin, trying to get as close to Megan as possible, trying to savor her scent, which Cole had to admit was intoxicating, a fine layer of sweet with an undercurrent of spice, unlike anything he'd ever encountered.

He waited, hoping to get a glimpse of her eyes again, to see if maybe he was wrong and there was an animal lurking somewhere inside, but she just kept her head down, shuffling things in the case, refusing to look at him.

"So you're Megan?"

She grunted.

"I'm Cole." He leaned against the counter and inhaled.

Human. Definitely human.

Ours, his cat rumbled again.

Okay, okay. Fine.

"So," Cole drawled out the word, trying to remember his plan. What was he supposed to be asking again? Something about trespassing. And naked dancing. He couldn't believe he'd missed seeing that!

Megan darted a glance at him, enough for him to see that she was perfectly human. Not a hint of an animal anywhere in her gaze.

Disappointing.

"If you don't need anything–" she began.

"A date," Cole blurted. "I-I mean, I was wondering if you'd like to go out sometime. To dinner."

Her hands stilled on a piece of jewelry, but only for a moment. If he hadn't been watching her so closely, he would have missed it.

"I'm busy."

Cole laughed. "I haven't suggested a time yet, so–"

"I'm *always* bus–"

"That sounds great!" Lara startled him as she bounded up and hooked arms with him.

He'd completely forgotten the other two women

were there, his attention had been so focused on Megan.

"She'd love to go out with you. How about tonight?" As Lara spoke, she turned them toward the door and started to walk him out.

"Lara!" Megan exclaimed behind them.

"You can pick her up at seven," Lara said cheerfully. "Does that work?"

"Um. Yeah, sure."

"Great!" Lara pulled open the door and practically shoved him out.

"All right, so I'll see you tonight, Megan!" Cole called as the door shut in his face.

~

Start reading Witchy Shenanigans today.
www.peppermcgraw.com/witchy-shenanigans

SHIFTER
Shenanigans

OTHER BOOKS BY PEPPER

THE MURRYSVILLE COALITION

The Crazy Cheetah Lady

One Sad Kitty

A PAWSITIVELY PURRFECT MATCH

Catnapped

The Real McCat

Unbearably Cute

A Catmas to Remember

This Cat's for You

Santa Kitty

Hocus Purrcus

Tridents & Tails

Abra-Cat-Abra

Satan's Kitty

Valen-Cats

Vampurr Lovin'

A Beautiful Cat-ship

Grave Cattitude

THE SHENANIGANS SERIES

Shifter Shenanigans

Witchy Shenanigans

Full Moon Shenanigans

Hotel Shenanigans

Dragon Shenanigans

Undercover Shenanigans

Spooky Shenanigans

Holiday Shenanigans

Valentine Shenanigans

Lucky Shenanigans

STORIES OF THE VEIL

Guardians of the Veil

Astra

Glory

Luna

Zara

WICKED

No Rest for the Wicked

Wicked Is As Wicked Does

STORIES OF THE VEIL

THE UNVEILED

Astra | Glory

THE VEILED

Luna | Zara

WICKED DUET

WICKED

No Rest for the Wicked | Wicked Is As Wicked Does